A DOG, A HORSE AND A HEART

Barbara Cartland

Barbara Cartland Ebooks Ltd

This edition © 2022

ISBNs

9781788676304 EPUB

9781788676311 PAPERBACK

Book design by M-Y Books
m-ybooks.co.uk

THE BARBARA CARTLAND ETERNAL COLLECTION

The Barbara Cartland Eternal Collection is the unique opportunity to collect all five hundred of the timeless beautiful romantic novels written by the world's most celebrated and enduring romantic author.

Named the Eternal Collection because Barbara's inspiring stories of pure love, just the same as love itself, the books will be published on the internet at the rate of four titles per month until all five hundred are available.

The Eternal Collection, classic pure romance available worldwide for all time .

THE LATE DAME BARBARA CARTLAND

Barbara Cartland, who sadly died in May 2000 at the grand age of ninety eight, remains one of the world's most famous romantic novelists. With worldwide sales of over one billion, her outstanding 723 books have been translated into thirty six different languages, to be enjoyed by readers of romance globally.

Writing her first book 'Jigsaw' at the age of 21, Barbara became an immediate bestseller. Building upon this initial success, she wrote continuously throughout her life, producing bestsellers for an astonishing 76 years. In addition to Barbara Cartland's legion of fans in the UK and across Europe, her books have always been immensely popular in the USA. In 1976 she achieved the unprecedented feat of having books at numbers 1 & 2 in the prestigious B. Dalton Bookseller bestsellers list.

Although she is often referred to as the 'Queen of Romance', Barbara Cartland also wrote several historical biographies, six autobiographies and numerous theatrical plays as well as books on life, love, health and cookery. Becoming one of

Britain's most popular media personalities and dressed in her trademark pink, Barbara spoke on radio and television about social and political issues, as well as making many public appearances.

In 1991 she became a Dame of the Order of the British Empire for her contribution to literature and her work for humanitarian and charitable causes.

Known for her glamour, style, and vitality Barbara Cartland became a legend in her own lifetime. Best remembered for her wonderful romantic novels and loved by millions of readers worldwide, her books remain treasured for their heroic heroes, plucky heroines and traditional values. But above all, it was Barbara Cartland's overriding belief in the positive power of love to help, heal and improve the quality of life for everyone that made her truly unique.

AUTHOR'S NOTE

The Setter hunting dog has been known and used in England for at least four hundred years.

The name 'Setter' is derived from the verb 'to set' which means to stiffen, position and point.

The name is therefore indicative of the role of the Setter as a pointing dog, although it adopts a different posture from the Pointer.

The Setter hunts with its head held high in order not to miss even the faintest scent of bird game.

The most ancient Setter breed is the English Setter and it has evolved over many years from crosses between the Spanish Pointer and Springer Spaniel.

It was first bred as a pet as well as a working dog by Sir Edward Laverack in the early nineteenth century.

The English Setter is an excellent hunting dog, good on any ground, whether it be flat land or marsh, woods or bush.

In appearance it is a attractive, elegant, well balanced dog and powerful without being heavy.

Its coat is long, silky, fine and slightly wavy, short on the head with abundant feathering at the legs.

The name 'Marquess' or 'Marquis' has the same meaning as Margrave, but this original significance has long been lost.

It was in 1385 that Robert de Vere, ninth Earl of Oxford, was created Marquis of Dublin with precedence established between Dukes and Earls.

This was resented by some other Earls and the Patent of the Marquisate was revoked on October 13th 1386 after its holder had been created Duke of Ireland.

John Beaufort, Earl of Somerset objected to being created a Marquis in 1402 because of the strangeness of the term in England.

On June 24th, 1443, however, his son Edmund Beaufort was raised to be Marquis of Dorset, after which the title retained its place in the Peerage.

CHAPTER ONE
1819

"I have sold that dog," the Earl pronounced

For a moment Manella looked at him in astonishment.

Then she asked,

"What do you mean. Uncle Herbert? You cannot have sold Flash? It could not be true!"

"Your father took him out shooting with Lord Lambourne one day last year, I am told, and Lambourne was extremely impressed that he was so fast and so obedient."

"My father was very fond of Flash," Manella then replied, "but he is *my* dog. He belongs to me."

Her uncle gave her a searching look before he asked her abruptly,

"You have that in writing?"

"No, of course not," Manella answered. "Is it likely that Papa would write down what he had given me? But Flash has always been mine and mine alone since he was a small puppy."

"You will not want him with you in London," the Earl said. "So Lambourne is coming to fetch him tomorrow afternoon."

Manella gave a cry that came from her heart.

"You cannot – you cannot do this to me, Uncle Herbert! I refuse to allow it and I will – not lose Flash."

The Earl of Avondale walked across the room to stand upright in front of the fireplace.

"Now, let us get this clear, Manella," he said. "Your father left very little money and you are now my responsibility. And you will appreciate that therefore I am doing what is best for you and will continue to do so to the best of my ability."

Manella did not reply and so her uncle went on,

"I have gone to a great deal of trouble already to arrange that you shall have a Season in London and then the Duchess of Westmoore will be chaperoning you."

Vaguely at the back of her mind, Manella recalled that the Duchess of Westmoore was very beautiful.

She had heard her father remark that his brother, Herbert, was making a fool of himself over her.

She did not say anything aloud and so the Earl went on,

"Most girls would be jumping for joy at the idea of being chaperoned by a Duchess. And I have also, I do believe, found you a husband."

Manella drew in a deep breath.

"I don't mean to be rude to you, Uncle Herbert," she said, "but I don't want my husband, when I have one, found for me. I wish to marry someone I love."

The Earl laughed and it was not a very humorous sound.

"*Beggars cannot be choosers*," my dear niece," he quoted for her benefit. "I happened to be in White's Club last week when the Duke of Dunster came into the morning room."

"The Duke of Dunster was a good friend of Papa's," Manella interposed.

"I do know that," he replied, "and I also know that he would give anything in the world to have a son to succeed him and inherit the Dukedom."

"I can hardly believe it that you should be – considering the Duke as my – husband," Manella said hesitatingly. "He is old – very old."

"What has that got to do with it?" the Earl enquired. "He is a Duke, he is rich and, if you are lucky enough to marry him, your whole future is completely made for you."

"I think you must be mad," Manella retorted, "if you think I would consider – marrying a man who is – old enough to be my – grandfather."

"I know the Duke has admitted that he can no longer shoot. But his son can do that, when he has one," the Earl replied, "Before you give me any more of your cheek, let me point out, Manella that, as I am your Guardian, you have to obey me and, if I tell you that you are to marry the Duke, you will marry him!"

"In which case you will have to drag me to the Altar – and I assure you that once I am there I will refuse to take part in the Marriage Service!" Manella countered furiously.

There was now an ominous look in her uncle's eyes as he went on,

"The trouble with you, Manella, is that you have been spoilt. You are a pretty girl, I will not argue about that. But unless you want to starve and be left without a penny to your name, you will do exactly what I tell you to do – and immediately!"

He walked slowly across the room to the door.

"I am going to inform Glover that Lord Lambourne will be here tomorrow afternoon. He will collect Flash and I hope I will be able to sell him at least two horses. The rest are only fit for the butcher."

He stalked out of the room as he finished speaking, slamming the door noisily behind him.

For a few moments Manella could only stare after him.

She could not believe what she had just heard and could not credit that it was the truth and she was not dreaming in a horrible nightmare.

How was it possible that her father's brother could behave in such a heartless and cruel way to her?

How could he take away Flash, whom she loved so much and who had been with her ever since he was born?

He had grown into a very fine and spirited Setter.

He was powerful but elegant. His white coat flecked with black was fine and silky and slightly wavy and he was greatly admired by everyone who saw him.

He followed her about the house, slept in her bedroom, and in fact went everywhere that she went.

It had never occurred to her when her uncle had said that they were going to London that she would not be able to take Flash with her.

Now she was not only going to lose the house where she had been born and where she had lived happily and contently ever since.

She was to lose Flash and Heron, the horse that she had always ridden and had believed was also hers.

She knew only too well that there were just the two horses in all of the stables that Lord Lambourne was likely to be interested in.

One of them was Heron.

On top of all this her uncle was now talking to her about her being married, but not to a man whom she might love and cherish.

He wanted her to marry a decrepit old man who wanted a wife only in order to have a son.

The horror of it all swept over her like a tidal wave and she wanted to scream and go on screaming.

Then she told herself that she must be calm and keep her self-control.

She must try to find some escape from this dreadful ghastly mist in which she felt that she was being suffocated by a cruel and harsh Fate.

She then looked up at the portrait over the mantelpiece, which was of her father.

It had been painted when he was a young man by one of the great artists of the time who had painted the Prince of Wales before he became the Prince Regent.

The sixth Earl of Avondale, her father, looked extremely distinguished and, as she told herself, very much the perfect gentleman.

It was something that her uncle certainly was not and never had been. It had often struck her in the past what an extraordinary difference there was between her father and his younger brother, her uncle.

She remembered once, when a large bill was sent to him because his brother had failed to settle it, her father saying,

"I suppose that there must be a 'Black Sheep' in every family, but Herbert is certainly proving himself blacker than most!"

Somehow the Earl had managed to pay his brother's debts and it was not for the first or the last time.

It was in point of fact largely due to Herbert's extravagance that they were so hard up.

The War against the French and Napoleon Bonaparte had certainly made everything very difficult for English families in all walks of life.

A number of those who had rented out their houses had left them because they were too large and expensive to run.

Or else they could not pay even the reasonable rent that the Earl was asking for

At the same time the farms did well because there were no foreign imports coming onto the market to compete with their produce

England therefore had to be self-supporting.

But, as soon as the War was over, the farmers began to feel the pinch and a number of County Banks had even closed their doors.

'If only Papa had not died just at this moment,' Manella thought to herself despairingly over and over again.

He had suffered an unexpected heart attack last autumn for no particular reason and had been able to hang on to life for only a few weeks.

Herbert, the 'Black Sheep', the ne'er-do-well, had then come into the title.

Because he had expected to have to wait many years before this happened, he had great difficulty in looking solemn and sad at his brother's funeral.

There had always been the possibility too that his brother might marry again and then go on to produce an heir.

But he himself was now the Earl!

As soon as the funeral Service was over, Herbert had started looking around the house for something to sell.

But most of the pictures and furniture were entailed onto each succeeding Earl, whoever he might be.

Herbert had said to Manella without the slightest hint of any embarrassment,

"I now have the opportunity of finding myself a rich bride."

Manella said nothing and he looked at her with a sneer on his lips as he added,

"You need not be so hoity-toity! You know as well as I do that your father was 'down to bedrock', which is something I myself have been now for years and years!"

He was silent for a moment or two before he went on,

"But then an Earl, poor or not, is a different story from a younger son with no prospects at all!"

"Then I would hope, Uncle Herbert," Manella said stiffly, "that you will find someone you can be really happy with."

"I will be happy with anyone providing she is rich enough," her uncle replied.

He had gone back to London, taking with him a number of items from the house that he intended to sell.

There was some *Sèvres* china that her mother had always been very fond of.

Manella tried her best to prevent him from removing it from the house.

"Now don't be so stupid," her uncle objected. "You know that I need money and it is for your benefit rather than mine that I intend to open up Avondale House in Berkeley Square."

Manella looked at him in astonishment.

"How can you afford to do that?" she asked. "Papa always said it was terribly expensive to keep up and needed a great number of servants."

"I am well aware of that," her uncle admitted, "but I shall be closing this house, leaving only a skeleton staff just in case I would wish to give a party here."

He saw the consternation in Manella's face and then added,

"So, of course, I shall have to impress my rich bride with the ancestral home of the Earls of Avondale."

He had stayed in London now for so long that Manella began to hope that what he had just been saying was a lot of nonsense.

Alternatively perhaps he was finding that it was not as easy to capture a rich bride as he had expected it to be.

Then yesterday he had returned unexpectedly and Manella felt herself shrink from him the moment he walked into the house.

He did not look in the least like her father and she had always thought that there was something insignificant as well as unpleasant about her uncle.

The moment he appeared she was aware that he was extremely smartly dressed.

He had arrived in a phaeton that looked new and expensive and the horses pulling it were well-bred.

She hoped, as he stepped in through the front door, that he had now found his intended rich bride-to-be.

Once that happened she thought that she would see as little of him as possible.

Now he had dropped a bombshell.

She found it difficult to think clearly after the shock of what he had just said.

Flash was lying on the hearthrug and she dropped down on her knees and put her arms around him,

"I cannot lose you – I *cannot*!" she said in a broken voice. "And I have always heard that Lord Lambourne is hard on his horses and his dogs. Oh, Flash, *Flash*, how could I – sleep at night if I thought you were in some – cold kennel and could not – understand why I was – not with you?"

It was then that the tears rolled down her cheeks and she brushed them away impatiently.

"I have to think of what we can do. Oh, Flash, tell me – what we can do."

Because the dog clearly understood that she was distressed, he licked her face.

Then he nuzzled her arm so that she put it round him.

She held him close and sighed through her tears,

"I cannot lose you – *I cannot*! If I have to – go to London and – marry some horrible old man – I will die!"

She thought even to herself that it all sounded too melodramatic and yet she knew that it was the real truth.

How could she live, knowing that Flash and Heron no longer belonged to her?

It was bad enough losing first her mother, then her father both of whom she had loved so much.

She had thought when he died that life stood still.

The future was dark.

But even in her worst fears of what her Uncle Herbert might do, it had never struck her for a moment that she would be separated from the two animals she loved more than anything else in the whole world.

Or that she would be taken to London to be disposed of to a husband he had chosen for her!

She was not even to be consulted.

'I will – not do it – *I will not*!" she declared again and again to herself.

She sat back on her heels and gazed forlornly up at her father's portrait.

Because of the way she had spoken and because she had released him, Flash thought it meant that they were going for a walk.

Jumping up he ran towards the door.

As he did so, Manella enthused,

"So you are telling me what to do! Oh, Flash, how clever of you! Why did I not think of that myself?"

She jumped to her feet and opened the door of the study.

Flash went out first, running ahead of her.

It was then that Manella began to plan her escape.

She was trying to keep calm and not be so apprehensive that she could not think clearly through the implications of her ideas and plans.

She fully realised that it would be a problem for her to earn enough money to live on her own.

She would also have to hide so cleverly that her uncle would never be able to find her however diligently he might search for her.

Manella went straight off to her bedroom and, then sitting down at the dressing table, she looked at herself in the mirror.

It was almost as if she was asking her reflection to guide her through all that beset her.

Manella had lived in the country all her life and during the War they had few neighbours and practically no parties.

She was therefore quite unaware of just how outstandingly pretty, in fact really lovely, she was.

She was completely unselfconscious about herself.

Soon after her father's death she had seen her uncle looking at her critically.

"You are making me feel uncomfortable, Uncle Herbert," she said, "Have I a smut on the end of my nose?"

"I was just thinking," the new seventh Earl of Avondale had replied slowly, "that you are a pretty young woman. In fact you compare favourably with the portraits of the Countesses of Avondale, who were always considered beauties in whichever period they lived."

Manella had been surprised by this, but she had responded a little shyly,

"Thank you, Uncle Herbert. I think that is the first compliment you have ever paid me."

He did not answer.

There was now a hostile look in his eyes that somehow made her feel apprehensive and uncomfortable.

She had the strange feeling that he was thinking that her looks were an asset in some way that she could not understand.

Now she realised that if she did have a rich and important husband, it would be an asset to him. An asset which was obviously of importance in Society, besides, of course, money.

How often, Manella remembered, had her father said,

"Why my brother wants to live in London, I just cannot imagine! But he has always been the same. Never cared for the country, never had any country interests and was always a bad shot."

That, Manella well knew, condemned him in her father's eyes.

He expected every English gentleman to enjoy the country and all the country sports and pursuits.

He should want to ride the best horses and shoot the highest birds.

Sometimes, when some of their relations came to stay, Manella would hear them talking to her father about his brother in low voices.

She had not been particularly interested at the time.

But, as they sat in one of the smaller rooms, if there was not a large party, she could not help overhearing their comments about Herbert's endless extravagance.

They also had a great deal to say about his many love affairs.

What concerned her father more than anything else was his brother's substantial debts.

The debts that were always brought to him for settlement when it was just impossible for Herbert to pay what he owed.

It was a question for the Earl of either finding the necessary money or letting Herbert rot in a Debtors' Prison.

Manella was aware of how much her father had suffered from this continual drain on the comparatively small amount of money he possessed.

It meant that he could not have the horses he wanted or that another gamekeeper had to be dismissed.

Or that urgent repairs to the house could not be undertaken even though the rain came through the roof regularly.

"Why do you keep doing this for Uncle Herbert?" Manella had asked her father once.

He had smiled somewhat drily as he replied,

"*Blood is thicker than water*, my dear, and, however tiresome Herbert may be, he is my brother and I have a deep regard for the family name."

This meant that he could not allow Herbert to go to prison as a debtor.

Manella knew that this was what her Uncle Herbert had always counted on.

'I hate him! *I hate him*!' she thought as she looked again at her reflection in the mirror.

She was thinking that she had somehow to earn enough money to live on and wondered what she could do.

Her hair was the pale gold of the sun in the early morning.

Her eyes, instead of being blue, as might have been expected because she was English, were the green of a woodland stream.

There was just a touch of gold in them which looked like the sun reflected on the running water.

One of the maids had once told her that she had a heart-shaped face.

When she looked at it, she knew that it was surely the truth.

Her eyes were very large and, strangely enough, her eyelashes were dark.

This was due, her father had always said, to a Spanish ancestress who had married one of the earlier Earls of Avondale.

Unfortunately there was no portrait of this particular Countess and Manella often thought it was sad that she had been omitted.

She thought that perhaps it was because the family had not liked her.

There was another foreigner who had more recently graced the Family Tree and that was Manella's grandmother, who had been French.

Manella had thought at the time how much it must have hurt her to know that her country was at War with her country of adoption.

However, according to her diary, she had been extremely happy.

She was not dark, as might have been expected, of a Frenchwoman but, having come from Normandy, she was fair. Only her eyes showed that she was definitely not English.

It was her grandmother who had taught Manella to speak French when she was small and because of this she found it as easy to read a book in French as one in English.

"I am sure, Grandmama," she had said when Napoleon was raging about the Continent and threatening to invade England, "that I should not speak the language of our enemy."

"You never know when it might come in useful," her grandmother had argued. "It is my opinion that the English make a great mistake in thinking they should not speak any language but their own. Whether they may like it or not, they have to associate with other countries in Europe in the future."

Manella had to admit that this was indeed true.

She therefore continued to speak French with her grandmother as she was fluent and to read books written in French that she lent her.

Her grandmother had gone out of her way to be especially kind to the French *émigrés* who had come to settle in England after the horrors of the Revolution.

Most of them had not returned home to France during the Armistice despite the fact that Napoleon had claimed that he would welcome them back.

When War had broken out again in 1804, they had been thankful that they had not taken advantage of his invitation.

"This man, Napoleon is an upstart, a discredit to his race!" Manella's grandmother had said scornfully.

She had always been very outspoken and in so many ways had a positive personality that was unusual.

Manella sat wondering how her grandmother would act in her present circumstances.

She was quite certain that she would not let herself be bullied into marrying anyone she did not wish to marry.

And she would certainly not agree to Flash being sold under any circumstances.

'But what can I do? How can I prevent it?' Manella asked her reflection despairingly.

'Flash is right,' she told herself finally. 'I shall have to run away.'

She spent the rest of the day trying to decide what she should take with her.

What was even more important was how she could put enough money together to save herself from starvation.

At least until she could find useful employment of some sort.

It was not going to be easy if she was to take Heron with her as well as her dog.

She could imagine what the housemaids at Avondale Hall would say if a servant arrived there with a well-bred horse and an outstanding Setter.

'I am sure that something will turn up,' Manella told herself consolingly.

At the same time she was feeling frightened and apprehensive.

There would doubtless be a tremendous fuss when she did run away.

Then if she was finally caught and returned home ignominiously, she knew just how her uncle would jeer at her.

He would keep her, having failed to become independent, triumphantly under his thumb.

She would have to do everything he ordered her to do.

Once again she thought of the Duke of Dunster and she shivered.

She remembered her father saying that he was now too old to take part in the shoots and that old men could often be a danger to the other shooters.

If indeed the Duke had been too old then, he was even older now.

How could she bear to be kissed or even touched by an old man with white hair?

Since her mother's untimely death, she had lived alone with her father.

So Manella was very innocent.

She had no idea what being married actually entailed.

She was, of course, aware that it was something intimate and that married people shared a bed together.

Her mother had been deeply in love with her father and he with her.

Whenever he had been away from home for a day and came back, her mother would run into the hall to greet him.

Regardless of the servants, who were in fact elderly and had been with them a long time, they would kiss each other lovingly.

Manella had been brought up in an atmosphere of love.

When she thought about marriage, which was not often, she imagined that the man she married would be tall and handsome like her father.

She would look at him and her face would glow, as her mother's did, so that she looked even more beautiful than she usually did.

"I have missed you," she had heard her father say once. "A day without you, my darling wife, is a very long day."

"And I have been counting the hours until your return," her mother had replied.

He had brought with him from

certain amount of wine as he had f

brother died that the cellars wer

He had also ordered the

something really decent

Manella overheard in

He had actually

the food with.

They had

he had g

had m

she would not wear a riding habit.

She wanted clothes that she could work in without feeling uncomfortable or restricted.

She still could not think of what sort of employment she might be able to find that would be interesting as well paid.

Yet when she went down the stairs to dinner with her uncle, she knew that, if she had to scrub floors and sleep in an attic, it would be far better than living with him or with a husband she did not love.

London a
ound when his
e almost empty.

servants to buy him
to eat for dinner as
urprise.

given them the money to buy

been only about scraping along since
one to London on the rabbits that they
anaged to snare in the woods.

There had been a duck or two which were to be found in the streams and the eggs that the chickens laid.

They roamed about in what had been known as the 'Kitchen Garden'."

They apparently had found enough vegetables and potatoes to eat there for it was very seldom that Manella could afford to buy any corn for them.

Somehow they had managed, although Manella was aware that she had lost a number of inches from her waist.

Emily, the housemaid, who was getting very old, had difficulty in sewing and grumbled when she had to take her gowns in.

Her uncle had also brought a *pâté* with him from London and then she felt that he was watching her carefully to see how much she took.

She therefore restricted herself to just a very small slice of it.

"I knew I would get little or nothing to eat here!" the Earl said scornfully. "But I have engaged an excellent cook for my house in Berkeley Square."

Manella could not help noticing the word '*my*'.

She knew exactly how much her father would despise his brother for closing their home in the country where the Earls of Avondale had lived for more than three hundred years.

Instead he was opening a house in London which was comparatively new, having been bought by his grandfather.

Her uncle, following his own thoughts, was boasting,

"I intend to give some very smart parties," he was saying, "and, of course, until you are married, you will help me to entertain."

He looked her up and down before he added,

"I suppose I shall have to find money for you to buy some decent clothes. You certainly cannot appear in Society as you are dressed now."

Manella raised her chin.

"Papa liked me in simple dresses," she said, "and, although this dress was made by the village seamstress, it is from a design that appeared in *The Ladies Journal*."

Her uncle gave a rude and rather vulgar laugh.

"If you will think that would 'pass muster' in the *Beau Ton*," he said, "then you are very much mistaken. In fact, if you want the truth, my dear niece, you look a mess! Your hair is not arranged in a fashionable way and your gown, if you appeared in it, would be laughed at from one end of Mayfair to the other!"

"I have no doubt you are right, Uncle Herbert," Manella said, "but Papa thought it wrong to buy anything unless we could afford to pay for it."

She hoped that she would make him feel uncomfortable, but instead he only laughed.

"Your father may have been well content to allow you to rot here amongst the turnips," he said. "But I am taking you into the real world, the world of important people who will be of use to us both."

Manella knew that he was speaking once again of the Duke and she felt herself stiffen.

Then her uncle said, looking at her in an appraising manner,

"Perhaps, after all, he will find it rather amusing to discover for himself that you are a beauty. At the same time we cannot afford to take the risk."

He paused before he repeated himself,

"No, it would be too great a risk. I must have you properly dressed, your hair arranged and perhaps a touch of salve on your lips to make them more inviting."

The way he spoke made Manella feel as if she was listening to the hiss of a serpent.

She wanted to rage at him that nothing would make her attempt to attract the Duke or any man who did not love her for herself.

Then she knew that it would be ridiculously pointless to say anything like that to a man who was so completely insensitive.

He looked at her merely as a means of benefiting himself and only himself materially.

Manella put down the cup of coffee that they had finished their dinner with.

"I think, Uncle Herbert," she said, "if you will excuse me, it would be correct for me to leave you to your port if you have any."

"I am glad you have been taught some of the conventions," the Earl replied. "However, I am quite certain that there are a great number that you do not know."

Manella rose to her feet.

"I hope you will forgive me, Uncle Herbert," she said, "if I now go to bed. I shall have a great deal to do in the morning if you are indeed thinking of leaving for London the day after tomorrow."

"I suppose you will have to take some of those old rags you are wearing with you," her uncle replied. "As soon as the Duchess has found you some decent clothes, we can burn the lot and a good thing too if you ask me!"

How dare he be so scathing, Manella thought.

It was almost entirely due to him that she had been unable to afford any new gowns for a very long time!

How dare he criticise her for being a 'country bumpkin' and so unlike the women who he amused himself with in London.

Women with whom he had caused, if she was not mistaken, scandal after scandal.

Pressing her lips together so as not to reply to him, Manella curtseyed politely and turned towards the door.

"Don't forget that Lambourne is coming tomorrow," her uncle said as she then went out of the dining room, "and you can give that dog a brushing. He looks as if he has just come out of the dustbin!"

Manella recognised that he was deliberately doing his best to provoke her.

Only as she then ran up the stairs with Flash at her heels did she say over and over again beneath her breath,

"I hate – him! I hate – him! *I hate – him!*"

CHAPTER TWO

The sun was just beginning to peep out over the horizon when Manella jumped out of her bed.

She had only slept for a very short while finding herself going over and over again in her mind what she had to do.

She dressed quickly, having the night before laid out the clothes she intended to put on.

She had wrapped those she was taking with her in a light shawl.

She had intended to take three of her simplest muslin gowns, which she hoped would not get too creased and would last her through the rest of the summer.

For the time being she gave no thought to what would happen in the winter.

Her riding habit was warm and would be all she wanted if it rained.

She had two pairs of shoes that fitted into Heron's saddle-pockets and a few other small articles that she knew she would need.

She had also late last night, when she thought that her uncle would be asleep, gone down to the armoury for one of her father's duelling pistols.

She was not so foolish as not to realise that she might be waylaid by highwaymen on her odyssey into the countryside.

She would be carrying very little of any value on her, but she was riding Heron and she had heard that highwaymen often took the best horses of anyone they held up.

Lastly, and it had taken her quite a long time to work it out, she had to have some ready money.

There was her mother's jewellery, which was beautiful, but not actually very valuable.

It was what her father had given her as presents and it always upset him that he could not afford more expensive surprises for her.

Her mother's engagement ring was of diamonds and there was also a diamond necklace that she had worn on special Society occasions.

The stones themselves were not that large or very fine, but if she was indeed becoming desperate, Manella thought, it would fetch enough money to last her for a good month or so.

What she lacked was actual cash.

She had only a few coins left from what she had been using as housekeeping money and she had lain awake thinking what on earth she could do.

Then she remembered that yesterday afternoon her uncle had given Mrs. Bell the cook several golden guineas.

This was not her wages, which were naturally overdue, but money to buy what he had called a 'proper meal' for Lord Lambourne.

"I have sent a groom to ask his Lordship to come to luncheon," he said. "I intend to give him a bottle of my best wine and I want you to serve a proper meal and not the rubbish you gave me last night and this morning, which is only fit for the pigs!"

Manella thought that it was a very unkind and unfair thing to say to poor Mrs. Bell.

She had done her best of late to provide them with food without spending a penny more than was absolutely necessary.

She saw the elderly woman flush, but she did not speak and her uncle said aggressively,

"Buy a leg of young lamb and some fresh cheese that does not look as if it is only fit for the rats!"

He paused for a brief moment before he added,

"I suppose we had better have some fruit as well. Strawberries or raspberries will do and I expect you will have to buy those too."

He then walked out of the kitchen as he finished speaking.

Manella realised at once that Mrs. Bell was muttering beneath her breath.

"I am sorry, Mrs. Bell," she said softly. "Uncle Herbert had no right to speak to you like that!"

"I've really done me very best, my Lady, as you well knows," Mrs. Bell said, "but I can't make bricks without straw and that be the truth!"

"Of course it is," Manella said consolingly, "but then we all know what Uncle Herbert is like."

She sighed before she went on,

"I suppose now that he has become an Earl he is able to borrow money, which he has not been able to do before."

She was speaking more to herself than to Mrs. Bell, but the elderly woman next informed her,

"I hears from the groom that's with his Lordship that he's got debts a mile long! But he's promised them, as he is askin' for a settlement that they'll all be met in under a month."

Manella stared at Mrs. Bell in astonishment.

"How is that possible?" she asked.

"The groom didn't know that. But he says that he thought it were somethin' to do with a Weddin'."

Manella started.

She knew only too well whose Wedding that would be.

As she had guessed, her uncle intended to put severe pressure on the Duke once he was her husband.

He would behave in exactly the same way as he had to her father.

He used to point out the danger of a scandal, which would affect the whole family.

He had been confident in his crafty cunning mind that his brother would pay up again.

Now, Manella thought, he intended to transfer these underhand methods to the Duke.

He would not want a scandal that was talked about in the newspapers that would involve his new wife as well as all the snide remarks from the Club members every time he went into Whites.

She now walked into the kitchen knowing where Mrs. Bell always kept the housekeeping money.

It was in a tin that stood on the dresser.

When she then pulled off the lid, she found, as she expected, that there were two golden guineas lying there untouched.

There was also quite a lot of small change and so she took it all, then put a note that she had already written to her uncle propped up on the dresser.

She wanted Mrs. Bell to find it there before she discovered that the money was missing.

The note was short and to the point and she thought for the moment that it would prevent her uncle from realising that she had run away.

She wrote,

"Dear Uncle Herbert,

After you had retired last night, I received a message from one of my friends inviting me to go and stay with her for a party they are giving tomorrow night.

As I am anxious to be present, I am riding over there on Heron. I am also taking Flash with me.

Lord Lambourne may be disappointed, but I expect you will be able to console him and he can always call another day.

As I needed some money to take with me, I have taken what you had given to Mrs. Bell for the food, so you must not blame her if you have to give her more for anything you may require.

I shall be returning soon, but it all depends on how long the party goes on for.

Yours,

Manella."

She deliberately did not put the letter into an envelope so that Mrs. Bell could read it before her uncle sent for her.

With the money in her pocket and the pistol, she slipped upstairs to her bedroom.

She reckoned that this would give her at least two, if not three days, to disappear in.

By then she must make it impossible for her uncle to find her wherever he may look.

At the same time, as she crept down the stairs with Flash at her side, she felt frightened.

She had always lived in this lovely house where she was born with her father and mother to protect her.

Now she was going out into a strange new world that she knew very little about.

If she had to come back ignominiously, she would be confronted not only by her uncle's anger but also by marriage to the Duke.

'I have to be successful – *I just have to*!' she thought as she went out through a side door towards the stables.

She knew that Glover would not be about at this time of the morning and the only help he had in the stables was his son of sixteen.

And he would be with him in his cottage tucked up in bed in a deep sleep.

There was, however, a new groom whom her uncle had brought with him from London. She had only just had a glimpse of him and thought he looked a rather unprepossessing man.

She had no trouble to find out where he slept.

It could be in the stables, as was traditional on large estates, or inside the house.

She wondered for a few minutes if he was aware that her uncle intended to sell Heron. If he did, he might make a scene about her taking the horse away so early in the morning.

Everything was quiet and peaceful in the stable yard.

When she entered the stable itself, there was only the sound of the horses moving in their stalls.

She glanced at the room at the end where the stable boys used to sleep in the past and to her relief it was empty.

This meant that her uncle's groom had been accommodated in the house.

Hastily, because she was afraid that somebody might appear, she saddled Heron and tied her bundle to the back of his saddle.

Then she opened the stable door as gently as she could.

She felt as if the sounds of his hoofs on the cobbles were alarmingly loud.

Then she knew that it was only because she was afraid that she would be prevented from leaving at the very last minute.

The sky was now brighter than when she had left the house and the stars were beginning to fade as dawn broke.

She took Heron to the mounting block.

Climbing onto it, she seated herself on the saddle.

She moved off, not going through the arch that led to the front of the house but out the back way.

Once they were in the open, Manella let Heron break into a trot.

At the same time she checked him from even cantering through the Park.

She realised that she must get as far away as possible and did not want him to be tired at the very beginning of her journey.

She also had to think of her faithful Flash. He was obviously so delighted to be going out and was running ahead and sniffing under every hedgerow for rabbits.

He was making it obvious that for him this was definitely a new and exciting adventure.

Manella wished that she could feel as equally elated as Flash.

One part of her brain told her that she was certainly doing the right thing under all the horrendous circumstances.

But her heart grieved at leaving her home, which was so full of memories of her beloved mother and father and, of course, her happy childhood.

Whilst she was there with them, she had always felt that they were looking after her as they had when she was a child.

Now she was grown up, on her own and facing a strange and frightening world all by herself.

She rode Westwards, knowing well in that direction there was pretty undulating country in which there were few houses and no one to notice her.

She had a distinct feeling, although she might be wrong, that her uncle, once he realised that she had run away, would think that she had gone Southwards.

Since London lay to the North, he would then assume that she would avoid the City at all costs.

She rode until the sun came out and, as it grew warmer, she tried to keep in the shade of trees and there were plentiful trees along her chosen route.

After about three hours it was becoming obvious that Heron was not as sprightly as he had been when they had started out.

He was now quite content to go slower at a gentle trot.

Flash too had ceased running ahead and quietly padded along behind.

Manella saw hardly anyone as she was now riding from field to field rather than moving along any of the country lanes.

This would have meant eventually passing through villages.

Manella was well aware of how curious villagers could be and a stranger always aroused comment, especially one riding a fine horse like Heron.

With Flash at her heels it would be certain that anyone who saw her would take notice and they would doubtless remember later that they had seen her passing by.

On and on they went deeper into the countryside until she realised that it must be nearly noon and that she was now feeling hungry.

Too late she thought that it was very foolish of her to have come away without any food and it would have been easy to have cut a large slice of her uncle's delicious *pâté* to take with her.

She had stopped twice already to let Heron and Flash drink from a clear stream.

At the last stop she had dismounted to hold her hands in the cool water and to splash it onto her face.

It was now very hot and becoming hotter all the time.

She began to think that she would be wise to stop and to take a rest.

At the same time she was very anxious to put as great a distance as was possible between herself and her uncle.

She reckoned that by now she had been riding for over six hours.

This meant that she was now no longer in a neighbourhood where anybody was likely to recognise her.

'I am safe – I am sure I am safe now,' she told herself reassuringly.

She then thought, however, that it would be a mistake to eat at an inn where she would undoubtedly be asked awkward questions.

The best thing would be to find a small village shop where she could perhaps purchase some slices of ham and beef.

Accordingly a mile or so further on she left the fields for a twisty lane and moving along it slowly.

As she expected, she soon saw ahead the roofs of some thatched cottages and the spire of a Church.

As she drew nearer, it all looked very quiet and peaceful.

The cottages had gardens in front of them which were bright with flowers and their doors and windows were well painted and in good repair.

She was not surprised a minute or two later to see the bow window of what looked like a prosperous village shop.

There was no one about in the street except for a few small children playing with a ball.

There was also a dog with them, who slouched away at the sight of Flash.

Manella rode up to the shop and dismounted.

She attached Heron's reins to a large wooden stump that had obviously been used before to tether horses whilst their owners were inside shopping.

With Flash at her heels, she then walked into the shop.

She had been right in thinking that it was a prosperous shop for she saw at a quick glance that there were a great many full shelves.

There was freshly baked bread on the counter and a ham that had recently been carved on a table behind it.

As she entered, a middle-aged man wearing spectacles and with a pleasant face rose from a chair were he had been sitting.

"Good mornin', ma'am," he greeted her, "and what can I do for you today?"

"I would like two slices of your ham, which I am sure is delicious," Manella answered, "and I was wondering if you, or perhaps there is a butcher in the village, could give me some scraps of meat for my dog?"

The shopkeeper peered over the counter at Flash.

"That be a fine lookin' dog you has there, ma'am," he remarked.

"He is a Setter," Manella replied.

The shopkeeper nodded as if he remembered that Setters were a special breed of Spaniel.

Then he started to sharpen a long thin knife before he cut in to the ham.

"What is the name of this pretty village?" Manella asked him.

Before he could reply to her question the door that she had entered the shop through was flung wide open.

A man who looked like a senior servant came bursting in.

"Mr. Getty! Mr. Getty!" he cried out. "There be a disaster up at The Castle and you're the only one as can help us!"

The shopkeeper put down his knife.

"A disaster, Mr. Dobbins?" he asked. "What can have occurred?"

"It be Mrs. Wade," Mr. Dobbins replied. "She's had a stroke! She is paralysed!"

"I don't believe it," Mr. Getty exclaimed. "How can it have happened?"

"She's bin complainin' about not feelin' too well," Mr. Dobbins replied, "I suspect it's worry over what to cook for his Lordship. It's been just too much for her."

Mr. Getty shook his head.

"She be gettin' on in years. And I've told her often enough that she should retire."

"She were that excited when she heard his Lordship were arrivin' today," Mr. Dobbins went on. "I have sent for the Doctor, but I knows even before he tell us so, there be nothin' we can do for her."

"I'm right sorry, indeed I am," Mr. Getty murmured.

"Well, what I've just come for," Mr. Dobbins replied in a different voice, "is to ask you if you knows of anyone as can take Mrs. Wade's place at least while we are lookin' around for someone else."

"Take her place?" Mr. Getty asked her. "Do you mean do the cookin'?"

"Course that's what I means," Mr. Dobbins responded. "With his Lordship arrivin' with three friends this evenin' and talk of more people comin' on Saturday."

Mr. Getty threw up his hands.

"That be enough for anyone to cope with and I knows only too well, Mr. Dobbins, there be nobody as can cook as well as our Mrs. Wade."

"That be the truth and no one can say different," Mr. Dobbins agreed. "But we can't have his Lordship sittin' down to an empty table! There must be someone in the village who you can suggest?"

Mr. Getty made a helpless gesture with his hands.

Then, as the two men stood looking at each other, Manella said without really thinking the implications through,

"I can cook!"

If the roof had fallen in the two men could not have been more surprised.

"You can cook, ma'am? You say you can cook?" Mr. Getty asked as if he did not believe her.

"Very well, as it happens," Manella answered. "In fact I had intended to ask you if there was anywhere that I could find employment in in this charming village."

For a moment there was complete silence as both men continued to gaze at her.

Then Mr. Dobbins said in a somewhat pompous manner,

"I think I should explain that his Lordship expects a very high standard of cookin'. Mrs. Wade were only sayin' yesterday that, havin' been in France for so long, he'd be expectin' some enticing French dishes as is not often seen in England."

"I am French by birth," Manella then pointed out, "and I have been able to cook French dishes of the sort that I expect you require since I was a child."

Mr. Getty put his hand up to his forehead.

"It certainly seems as if you've struck it ever so lucky, Mr. Dobbins," he said. "Who'd have thought that a lady as was buyin' two slices of ham from me could cook in the French fashion?"

Mr. Dobbins wanted reassuring.

"You are quite certain," he said, "that you can cook French dishes, as you say you can? It'd be embarrassin' like if his Lordship was served up inferior food when he's payin' us a visit for the first time after bein' so long abroad with the Army."

"What is his Lordship's name?" Manella then asked.

Mr. Dobbins took a deep breath.

"He be the Marquis of Buckingdon and that's where you are at the moment in the village of Buckingdon, which, of course, belongs to his Lordship."

Manella's eyes widened.

She had indeed heard of the Marquis of Buckingdon. Who had not?

After the War was now finally over, the Duke of Wellington had publicly praised all of those who had served under him so bravely and so successfully.

He had then specially mentioned the Earl of Buckingdon, who had commanded one of his crack Regiments.

It had been a spectacularly successful soldier in all theatres of the War.

By brilliant tactics and expertise the Earl had saved the lives of many men who otherwise would have perished at the hands of a ruthless enemy.

Later, when the period of Occupation had ended, the Prince Regent gave a special party just for the Earl.

The highlight of the evening had been when His Royal Highness had appointed him a Marquis for his splendid achievements in the War.

The reason why Manella had been interested in the reports of this in the newspaper was that her father had often spoken of the Marquis's father. They had been at Eton together and only lost touch when her father had no longer been able to afford to travel to London.

He had also stopped attending shooting parties at which the tenth Earl of Buckingdon would undoubtedly have been a guest.

When the Earl died, her father had sent a wreath, but had not felt well enough to attend his funeral.

She remembered too that when Napoleon was finally defeated, it was the eleventh Earl of Buckingdon who had been Wellington's Right-Hand Man with the Army of Occupation.

At one time there seemed to be hardly a day when he was not mentioned in *The Morning Post* in glowing terms.

It was the only newspaper that her father ever bought.

Then, when the Occupation finally came to an end, there were no further eulogies about the new Marquis.

He was then only mentioned in *The Court Circular* that was by no means so interesting.

Manella thought that it might be exciting to cook for the man who had stood out as such a legendary hero among his contemporaries.

She therefore said quickly,

"I have heard of his Lordship and I promise you that he will not be disappointed in my cooking even though he has spent several years away in France."

"There you are, Mr, Dobbins," Mr. Getty said. "No one can say fairer than that. If you asks me, you were born under a lucky star, findin' somebody as can cook just at the moment when you really needs it."

"I agree with you." Mr. Dobbins smiled.

He turned to Manella.

"Are you prepared, miss, to come up to The Castle with me right away?"

He hesitated before he addressed her as 'miss' and Manella saw him glance at her hand to see if she was wearing a Wedding ring.

She was just about to acquiesce and confirm that she would go with him when Flash moved beside her.

"There is one condition I must make, Mr. Dobbins," she said, "and that is if I come and cook for the Marquis, I can bring my horse and my dog with me."

She thought that there was a look of incredulity on Mr. Dobbin's face.

Then, because he was so desperate, he answered her confidently,

"Of course. That'll be all right! There's plenty of room in the stables at The Castle."

Manella smiled.

"Then I will gladly come with you," she said.

She held out her hand to Mr. Getty.

"It has been a pleasure to meet you," she said, "and, although I will not now require your delicious ham, perhaps I can come for some another day."

"You'll be very welcome here, miss," Mr. Getty said with a grin.

Mr. Dobbins opened the door and Manella stepped out into the sunshine.

As she walked towards Heron, he followed her.

"That be a fine horse you have there, miss," he said admiringly, "very fine!"

"Thank you," Manella replied.

She was aware that there was a note of curiosity in his voice.

It was obvious that he was wondering why, with a horse like that, she should be looking for employment.

Then unexpectedly he enquired,

"Will you please tell me your name? I, as you know, am Mr. Dobbins and I am butler to his Lordship."

It was what Manella had expected and she was wondering what she should reply.

Then she told herself that if her uncle was indeed making enquiries as to where she was, he would not expect that she would have described herself as 'French'.

The first French name that came into her head was her grandmother's.

"My name, Mr. Dobbins," she said rather slowly, "is Chinon. It is, of course, French and although I have lived all my life in England, my parents came over before the Revolution."

She felt safe in saying that because a great number of *émigrés* had fled from France and it would explain how she knew so much about French cooking.

Mr. Dobbins thought for a moment.

Then he said,

"If you'll excuse me sayin' so, you looks too young to be a cook and too young to have anythin' to do with the Revolution. It'd be best therefore to introduce you to the household as 'Miss Chinon' and not go into any details as to how you can cook in the French fashion."

He mispronounced the name.

It was also obvious he thought that for the Marquis to have a cook who was really French could be embarrassing.

She smiled at him and said,

"I am delighted to be called 'Miss Chinon' – and thank you, Mr. Dobbins, for being kind enough to employ me."

Mr. Dobbins had driven from The Castle in a small cart drawn by a well-bred horse.

It was standing not far from Heron and was obviously well-trained and, despite the fact that it was not secured, it had made no effort to move away.

Mr. Dobbins climbed into the cart saying,

"Follow me, Miss Chinon."

Manella managed to climb up into Heron's saddle.

As she rode after Mr. Dobbin's cart, she waved to Mr. Getty who was watching them go.

She was not surprised to find that along one side of the road there was a high wall that obviously enclosed the grounds of The Castle.

They had not gone that far before they came to some imposing wrought-iron gates tipped with gold and flanked on either side by a lodge.

The butler then drove his cart through the entrance and Manella followed him down an avenue of imposing oak trees.

As she did so, she thought that she had been extraordinarily fortunate.

If nothing else she at least had a bed for the night for herself and a stable for Heron.

She hoped fervently that she would not disappoint the Marquis or Mr. Dobbins, who had trusted her when she told him that she could cook.

It was her grandmother who had taught her French cooking.

"When I was a girl," the Countess had said, "my mother insisted on my learning all the most delicious and traditional French dishes to please my father."

She smiled before she went on,

"When I married your grandfather, he used to ask me sometimes to cook him one of my special French dishes, which no English cook could manage however hard they tried."

"What is the secret of French *cuisine*, Grandmama?" Manella had asked.

"That is what I am going to teach you," her grandmother promised.

Manella found it fascinating to create dishes that were so very different from the English fare as provided by Mrs. Bell.

Sometimes, when her father had been away for a night or even just for a day, her mother would say,

"Let's give Papa a treat, my dearest, and cook him something special to show that we are glad to have him home again and we still love him as much as ever."

Rather like conspirators they would then hurry down to the kitchen.

As her grandmother had taught her to cook so well, both her mother and Mrs. Bell would watch her.

They were fascinated as she prepared one or two French dishes that were very different from what they usually ate.

Manella told herself now that she had never imagined for a moment that she would ever become a professional cook.

As if Fate was taking a hand in her destiny, the position had been there waiting just for her when she least expected it.

As she rounded the drive, the magnificent Castle came into sight.

It was just the sort of house, she thought, which the Marquis with all his Honours should live in. It was very large and the Great Tower of the original Castle was still standing.

Manella was to learn later that it had been built after the Battle of Agincourt in 1415. In the previous century the remains of The Castle had been converted and added to in order to create an enormous Palladian mansion.

From a tall centre block there jutted out an East wing and a West wing and the East wing connected with the old Castle.

The house now had over a hundred windows all glittering in the afternoon sunshine.

The courtyard in front of it sloped down to a beautiful lake, which was spanned by an ancient bridge.

The gardens around the house were ablaze with flowers and shrubs.

Behind The Castle stood trees on rising ground, which made a spectacular background like a setting for a precious jewel.

In fact the house was so lovely that Manella felt that she must be imagining it and at any moment it would disappear in a puff of smoke.

'I am so lucky!' she told herself yet again.

She bent forward to pat Heron's neck.

"And you are lucky too," she said. "I am quite certain that if the Marquis lives in such comfort and luxury, your stable will be comfortable too."

As they passed over the bridge, Manella found herself saying a little prayer of thanks.

'Thank You, God – thank – You!' she whispered. 'I am feeling very sure that Uncle Herbert will never find me here!'

CHAPTER THREE

When Mr. Dobbins and Manella arrived at The Castle, they entered the house through the front door.

This, Manella thought, was a concession because the Marquis was not at home and she was new.

She was tremendously impressed with the marble hall with its Greek statues standing in alcoves and there was a magnificent marble mantelpiece. The staircase had alternating gold and crystal stair-rails and it curved upwards towards an exquisitely painted ceiling.

Manella had left Heron with a groom, but Flash had followed her into the house.

The butler glanced at him before he said,

"I'll go and find the housekeeper, Miss Chinon, and I suppose that your dog has always lived in the house with you?"

"Yes, he has," Manella answered firmly. "And he sleeps every night by my bed."

She thought that Mr. Dobbins then looked slightly apprehensive at this revelation.

He went ahead of her up the stairs.

As they then reached the landing, Manella saw a most impressive figure coming down the corridor

It was The Castle's housekeeper in rustling black silk with a huge silver chatelaine at her waist.

"Good afternoon to you, Mrs. Franklin," the butler said. "I've brought you a new cook for his Lordship!"

"A new cook?" the elderly housekeeper exclaimed in astonishment.

She was looking at Manella as she spoke and said before Mr. Dobbins could speak,

"Surely you don't mean this young lady?"

"I do indeed!" Mr. Dobbins affirmed. "And she's assured me and Mr. Getty that she's a very good cook, in fact she's especially proficient in French dishes."

Mrs. Franklin looked doubtful.

"I promise you," Manella said in a quiet voice, "that I really am an excellent cook and I am confident that his Lordship will be more than satisfied."

"If that is so, then we're ever so lucky!" Mrs. Franklin insisted.

At the same time she was very obviously somewhat sceptical that this strange and far too pretty young woman was speaking the truth.

"Now what we have to find, Mrs. Franklin," Mr. Dobbins said briskly, "is a room where Miss Chinon can have her dog with her."

"Her dog?" Mrs. Franklin exclaimed at once. "We never allow the staff to have pets of their own."

There was an uncomfortable pause until Manella said quietly,

"Flash has been with me ever since he was a puppy. He is perfectly house-trained and, as I have explained already to Mr. Dobbins, I just cannot stay here and cook for you unless I can have both my horse and my dog with me."

Manella saw Mr. Dobbins look at Mrs. Franklin frantically and then realised that she was acquiescing.

"Very well, Miss Chinon," she said. "If you'll come with me, I'll find you a room."

It was then that Manella remembered that she had left her clothes on Heron's saddle.

"I am sorry, Mr. Dobbins," she said next, "but please would you be very kind and send someone to fetch the bundle that is attached to my horse's saddle? There are also some shoes in the pockets."

"I'll do that, Miss Chinon," Mr. Dobbins said, "and thank you. Thank you very much for helping us out of our present difficulties."

He gave Mrs. Franklin a sharp look.

He obviously was warning her not to upset Miss Chinon since otherwise they would find themselves without a cook of any description.

As he went down the stairs, Mrs. Franklin, realising that Mr. Dobbins was right, said in a different tone of voice,

"I think it would be wise, Miss Chinon, not to put you with the other staff at the top of the house as you have a dog with you. It might give them ideas and I have a horror of having to tolerate someone's cat or, as one housemaid wished to bring with her some years ago, a white rabbit."

Manella laughed.

"I can well understand, Mrs. Franklin, that you have no wish to have a menagerie in this beautiful house. At the same time I just cannot be separated from my adorable dog."

"His late Lordship, God rest his soul, felt the same," the housekeeper said. "His Spaniels went everywhere with him and they were well trained and very well-bred."

"You must be very proud of the Marquis," Manella remarked. "Although I come from a different part of the country altogether, I have read about his bravery in the War and what His Royal

Highness the Prince Regent said about him when he awarded him his Marquisate."

"We're indeed real proud of his Lordship," Mrs. Franklin agreed at once. "And he were the nicest little boy as ever was."

She walked on down the corridor until she opened the last door with one of the many keys at her waist.

"This is a room that is very seldom used," she said, "except when we're so full that all the larger rooms on this floor are taken."

It was indeed a pleasant enough bedroom, Manella thought, but obviously intended for a bachelor.

There was no dressing table just a mirror over the chest of drawers and the oak wardrobe had a masculine look about it.

There was what appeared to be a comfortable bed and a large window overlooking the front of the house and the lake.

"This will suit me perfectly," Manella said, "and thank you for being so *understanding*."

She emphasised the word and Mrs. Franklin knew that she was referring to Flash.

"Now, if there's anythin' you would want ask me," she said. "For the moment, however, I'm sure you will want to see the kitchen, as there's so very little time to make preparations before his Lordship's arrival."

Manella took off the small hat that she was wearing and put it down on a chair.

Pushing her golden hair into place, she then said,

"I am quite ready to start and, of course, I realise that there is a great deal of work ahead of me."

Mrs. Franklin took her down a side staircase to the ground floor.

They passed the pantry, which she could see was quite large and she knew it was where a footman would sleep at night in order to guard the safe and its valuables.

Mrs. Franklin, who was moving ahead, opened a door that led into the kitchen.

It was, as Manella had expected, a large room with a high ceiling and there were beams with hooks on which to hang food.

It was something that she could always remember seeing when she was no more than a child.

There was a ham, several ducks, a number of pigeons and some onions tied together by their stalks.

She walked towards the huge stove where, standing beside it and stirring something in a saucepan, was a girl of about sixteen.

Another girl of the same age was next to her shelling peas.

They looked up at her in some surprise.

"Bessie and Jane will help you, Miss Chinon," Mrs. Franklin said. "I'm afraid they're very young, but Mrs. Wade was teachin' them to do things the way she liked and found that older women we had previously were too slow."

"l am sure they will be a great help," Manella said smiling at them.

The two girls smiled back shyly.

"I don't know what they've prepared for luncheon," Mrs. Franklin said, "but I suggested before Mrs. Wade was took ill that, as there'd be so much to cook for tonight, we'd best have somethin' cold."

"I think that is a very good idea," Manella said. "And I can see that there is a ham at any rate."

She pointed up to the beam from which ham was suspended.

"There should be a good deal more than that," Mrs. Franklin replied. "What's happened to the chicken you was cookin' yesterday, Bessie?"

"If be in the larder, Mrs. Franklin," Bessie replied.

"Then run and fetch it, child, *fetch it!*" Mrs. Franklin ordered. "And anything else that Miss Chinon can give us to eat."

As Bessie hurried away, Manella remembered what her home had been like when her mother was alive.

"I suppose," she said, "you and Mr. Dobbins have your luncheon in the housekeeper's room, Mrs. Franklin? And the kitchen staff and housemaids and footmen eat in the servants' hall."

"That's right," Mrs. Franklin agreed.

She spoke with an expression of approval in her eyes.

She accepted now that Manella knew just how a gentleman's household was organised and arranged.

"And you, of course," Mrs. Franklin added, "will have your meals with Mr. Dobbins and myself."

"I am sure the girls will have prepared some vegetables," Manella said, "and I will have luncheon sent to the housekeeper's room as quickly as possible."

"That be very helpful of you, Miss Chinon," Mrs. Franklin replied.

She swept out of the kitchen with a rustle of her silk gown.

When she had gone, Manella smiled again at the two girls.

Bessie had just come back carrying a tray with the cold chicken on one plate and a large sirloin of beef on another.

"Personally I am hungry!" Manella said. "While I finish off the vegetables that you have been cooking, I should be very grateful if you, Bessie, would cut me a slice of chicken and if Jane will get down that ham which is hanging up overhead."

The girls hurried to obey her and she ate some of the chicken as she put the vegetables into china dishes.

She also gave several small pieces to Flash who was sitting hopefully under the table.

She was thinking that, however busy she might be, she must go to the stables to see that Heron was all right and happy in his new home.

She felt sure that there would be sufficient water in his stall and a good feed of oats.

She could not believe that the Marquis, of all people, would ever skimp on his horses.

What mattered at the moment more than anything else was that neither Heron nor Flash should go hungry.

By the time the afternoon was drawing to a close Manella had everything prepared for dinner.

She had not been so foolish as to start by making French dishes the moment she arrived.

She had to have the correct ingredients for one thing and, for another, to get to know her way completely round the kitchen.

She did not go to the housekeeper's room for her luncheon. Instead she ate in the kitchen alone after the girls had gone to the servants' hall.

Manella learnt that there were six footmen, five under-housemaids and the two girls in the kitchen to feed as well as the senior staff.

There was also one old man who she gathered brought in the coal and the wood for the fires.

She had sent a message to Mrs. Franklin knowing that the butler and housekeeper would understand that she had too much to do to join them at present.

She had just finished her luncheon and was beginning to think that the cold chicken and the home-cured ham tasted delicious because she was so hungry.

It was then that Mr. Dobbins came in to join her.

"I forgot to tell you, Miss Chinon", he said as he came into the kitchen, "that Mrs. Wade has prepared dinner for tonight and the menu has already been written out by his Lordship's secretary."

"That is what the girls have told me," Manella replied, "and I therefore intend tonight to serve exactly what Mrs. Wade had planned."

She thought that Mr. Dobbins gave a sigh of relief. He must have thought that it would be difficult in those circumstances for her to go wrong.

He then said,

"In the excitement of bringing you back here in triumph, Miss Chinon, I also forgot that you should have seen Mr. Wilson, his Lordship's secretary, before you started work in the kitchen. He would like to talk to you now about the position and to discuss your salary."

"Thank you," Manella said, "and perhaps you would be kind enough show me the way."

She was taken by Mr. Dobbins through what she thought was a labyrinth of passages.

Eventually they came to the secretary's room on the other side of the house.

Mr. Wilson was an elderly man who she learnt subsequently had been at The Castle with the Marquis's father ever since he had inherited.

When she was introduced to him by Mr. Dobbins, he stared at her in astonishment.

Then he quizzed her,

"You are really a cook, Miss Chinon?"

"I really am," Manella said, "and I know that you are being polite in not adding that I look too young."

"It had certainly crossed my mind," Mr. Wilson admitted.

"I do not think you will be disappointed," she replied. "But, of course, if you are, I need only stay until you can find another cook."

"I feel sure that is something I will not have to do," Mr. Wilson replied gallantly,

Mr. Dobbins withdrew and Manella sat down in a chair opposite the desk.

"Now I have to ask you what wages you are asking and, I appreciate, Miss Chinon, that you have saved us from being in a most uncomfortable situation at what I might say was 'the eleventh hour'."

Manella laughed.

"If you are suggesting I am going to blackmail you, I will not do that, Mr. Wilson. I will accept very gratefully whatever you consider is a fair wage for me."

Mr. Watson somewhat tentatively told her what salary Mrs. Wade was receiving.

Manella accepted it without further discussion. She thought that, if she stayed only a few weeks, it would bring her enough money for her to proceed on her way without being afraid that Heron and Flash would go hungry at any stage.

When she rose from her chair, she held out her hand to Mr. Wilson.

"Thank you so much," she said. "You may be grateful that I have appeared unexpectedly when you were in such difficulties, but I also am grateful to you because I was looking for a position and was not quite sure how quickly I would be able to find one."

"I can only hope, Miss Chinon, that you will be happy here with us," Mr. Wilson smiled.

Manella hurried back to the kitchen.

She thought that everything was going very well so far, the only difficulty now would be if the Marquis disapproved of her.

Then she told herself that she was very unlikely to come into any direct contact with him.

And any comment he had to make about her cooking would be conveyed to her by the butler.

She then started to work hard to get everything ready for the dinner party.

There were to be five courses, starting with soup and ending with a savoury.

Manella knew all the relevant recipes very well and would most certainly not forget even the smallest detail.

The planned menu was what Mrs. Bell would always have considered to be exactly the 'right food' for presenting at a dinner party or a special occasion.

She was an excellent cook in that everything tasted just as it should.

She had not, however, been particularly imaginative and sometimes Manella had longed for the delicious French dishes that her grandmother had taught her to make.

Then she would go into the kitchen and say to Mrs. Bell,

"I have nothing much to do today so I have come to help you."

"You don't deceive me with that honeyed talk, my Lady," Mrs. Bell would reply sharply. "You're after makin' that 'Froggy' food! You should be ashamed to eat it when that wicked man, Napoleon, has killed so many of our dearest kith and kin."

It was something that she always said and never tired of repeating it.

At the same time she would let Manella make *Crêpes Suzettes* or a *Strawberry Sorbet* and even commended her on how delicious it was when she had done so.

'Tomorrow night,' Manella told herself, 'I will give his Lordship a treat.'

Manella cooked the English menu perfectly just as Mrs. Bell would have done.

It was taken into the dining room solemnly by Mr. Dobbins and his footmen.

Mr. Dobbins came back smiling.

"His Lordship be enjoyin' himself," he said, "and so's the Lady he's brought with him."

"Lady?" Manella enquired.

"That's right," Mr. Dobbins said, "and 'she be a Frenchy, believe it or not, just like you!"

"What is her name?" Manella asked.

"Her be the Comtesse d'Orbrey." Mr. Dobbins pronounced her name rather strangely, "and he calls her 'Yvette'."

Manella was surprised that the Marquis would be entertaining anyone who was French.

Then she felt that he had doubtless met her when he was with the Army of Occupation in Paris.

"And who are the gentlemen?" she enquired.

"One calls himself a 'Comte' and he seems to be her brother," Mr. Dobbins replied. "His name's a bit queer, 'de Fuisse', I think it is, and the other be just a 'Monsieur'."

"And again French?" asked Manella.

"From Paris he said he was," Mr. Dobbins answered. "An ugly-looking man, but then he seems to amuse his Lordship."

"Well, as long as they are satisfied with the dinner, that is all that matters," Manella said.

"They certainly eats it all!" Mr. Dobbins assured her. "And suckin' up they were to his Lordship and hangin' on every word he said, especially the Comtesse."

Manella was not particularly interested in the Marquis's guests.

She was wondering if she would have a chance to actually see him.

Then she reminded herself that her one bedroom window looked out over the front of the house.

If by no other way, she would see him mounting his horse outside the front door or even driving a phaeton.

She was by this time feeling very tired.

She had hardly slept at all during the night before and worrying how she could get away from her uncle.

As soon as the kitchen was tidy, she sent the two girls to bed.

She was determined to follow them as soon as possible.

She had, however, to take Flash out for a walk first and so she took him out by the back door.

'Tomorrow,' she reflected, 'I must explore The Castle and find out where everything is. But for the moment I must just be content to know that I have a comfortable bed to sleep in that I don't have to pay for.'

There were some bushes near to the back door and between them there was a path lined with shrubs.

As the moon was rising in the sky, it was easy to see where she was going.

She walked along the path and found shortly that it led to the stables.

She knew then that she realised that she could not possibly go off to bed without seeing Heron again and so she entered the stables.

There was a long row of doors and she went in and opened the first one.

By the light on the wall she could see to her delight that the horse's stalls were roomy and comfortable.

She passed a number of horses before she eventually came to where Heron was stabled.

Going into his stall she put her arms round his neck and he nuzzled up against her.

"We are safe, my darling," she said. "We are here and I don't believe Uncle Herbert or anyone else could ever guess where I am."

She felt as if Heron, whom she had always talked to, understood every word that she was saying.

She patted him and made a great fuss of him and then saw that his manger was full of the most expensive oats.

There was also a full bucket of fresh water beside him for him to drink.

She went back to the house followed by Flash.

The kitchen was in darkness and the only sound was coming from the pantry.

She slipped past without being noticed and went up the side stairs to the first floor.

The guests, she knew, would all be occupying the State rooms that she had not yet seen and they were all further along the corridor.

When she went back into her own room, it seemed like a haven of peace.

She knew that for tonight at any rate she would be able to sleep without being afraid.

Flash made himself at home by settling down comfortably beside the bed.

As Manella undressed and patted him before she said her prayers, she told herself that she was seriously very lucky.

*

The following morning Manella awoke with a start.

When she looked at the clock on the mantelpiece, however, and she found that it was not yet six o'clock.

It was a relief because she had forgotten to tell one of the girls to call her and was afraid that she might have overslept.

She then hurried down the stairs to prepare breakfast.

She was next informed that his Lordship required breakfast at eight o'clock.

"He's goin' ridin'," a footman informed her, "but tomorrow he'll ride early and have his breakfast after he returns to the house."

"Well, as long as I am warned, I can have everything ready," Manella answered.

She was thinking as she cooked that she must somehow find time to exercise Heron.

She felt that it would be a very good thing for him to have a quiet day today having been ridden so far yesterday.

But then he was young and incredibly spirited.

He would soon grow restless if she did not ride him regularly as she always did.

'But if the Marquis rides early,' she calculated, 'I shall have to go out earlier still or else slip away from my duties in the afternoon.'

She felt sure that once luncheon was over the servants would expect to take it easy until teatime.

If she prepared the sandwiches and the baked the cakes beforehand for tea they would be ready to be taken from the kitchen into the drawing room when called for.

'I have to plan out my work properly,' Manella told herself severely. 'It would be a great mistake to overlook something I ought to be doing the moment I have arrived here.'

She therefore then concentrated on preparing the breakfast, making six different dishes for the dining room.

She put the eggs, fish, mushrooms and kidneys that Mrs. Wade had left ready into silver serving dishes and they were kept warm by means of lit candles fitted underneath them.

At the last moment she realised that she had forgotten last night to put a loaf of bread in the oven so that it would be ready for the morning.

'They will have to manage with just toast,' she told herself, 'but it is something I must not forget to do again.'

She could have blamed the girls for not reminding her.

But she knew that they themselves had not been employed at The Castle for very long.

Naturally they could not therefore be expected to know how people like the Marquis's friends expected things to be done.

'I must remember exactly how we used to do everything at home,' Manella told herself as the past started to come back streaming back to her mind.

It made her appreciate just how much things at home had deteriorated after her mother's death.

As, all thanks to Uncle Herbert, they became poorer and poorer, one luxury after another had disappeared and was eventually forgotten.

While she was putting together what was required for luncheon, she then started to think about what she would give the Marquis and his guests for dinner that evening.

It was beginning to dawn on her just how exciting it was to think that she could make the French dishes that her grandmother had taught her so brilliantly without then having to worry about the expense.

She could now choose the large number of ingredients that had been set aside at home as being too extravagant.

Finally she had her menu all prepared.

When the gamekeepers and the gardeners came into the kitchen for her orders, she told them exactly what they had to find.

"We'll do our extra best, miss," they said scratching their heads, "but it ain't goin' to be easy."

"I know," Manella smiled. "But none of us can do enough for his Lordship, can we?"

It was exactly the right note to strike.

They all agreed at once that 'the Marquis deserved the best' and no mistake about it.

By teatime Manella had everything prepared. When she learnt that the Marquis and his friends were sitting comfortably in the drawing room, she thought that she might well explore a little more of The Castle.

She had also learnt that more of the Marquis's friends were arriving the next day and the housemaids had been told that eight more bedrooms were to be made ready for them.

The grooms were expecting three or four carriages and had to see to the stabling.

The housemaids were all busy preparing for the new guests and the servants they would bring with them.

Manella thought that she could now that safely slip away from all this frenzied activity. She had decided that she would like to go first to the music room and after that she would go to the library and the ballroom.

She had eaten luncheon with Mrs. Franklin in the housekeeper's room and she had learnt how much there was to see and admire in The Castle.

"I expect you'll enjoy all the paintings in the Picture Gallery," the housekeeper told her. "And when you're lookin' at them, remember it's us as has to keep the floor polished and that's a real task, I can tell you!"

The Curator, who was an old man and who had also lunched with them, told Manella he would show her the books in the library.

Some, he related to her, were first editions and so were very valuable and much sought of by avid collectors.

She thought it unusual for a Curator to have his meals in the housekeeper's room, but he said he felt lonely and enjoyed a good chat while he was eating.

Mr. Wilson, he said with pleasure, was unfortunately only interested in mathematics and finance!

Manella had laughed,

Yet she understood why Mr. Wilson had his meals taken to him on a tray by one of the footmen.

That was another item that she had to prepare in the kitchen and because she felt sorry for him, she tried her very best to make his dishes look as appetising as possible and so she decorated them in a way that was certainly more French than English,

She decided not to visit the library yet, because she knew that the Curator would want to keep her talking to him when she was so busy preparing and cooking.

Then there would be no time to see the rest of the rooms that she so wanted to visit.

She therefore went first to the music room, which was fascinating. There were classic murals on the walls and a very impressive ceiling.

The ballroom, which had not been used since before the War, was awe-inspiring.

With the chandeliers lit and the room filled with flowers, it could be the most romantic room that she had ever seen in her life.

She had been told by Mrs. Franklin that there was no one sleeping in the East wing.

And she was wondering whether she had time to explore that part of The Castle.

Then she decided that she must leave that pleasure for another day.

She, however, looked at the huge oak door that separated it from the newer part of The Castle.

As she did so, she became aware of another door and, as she was curious, she opened it.

She found that it led to a Chapel.

Because it was situated between the ancient door and the new building she guessed that it was as old as the original Castle.

It was certainly a very lovely Chapel with stained-glass windows and carved pews that were obviously hundreds of years old.

There was a cloth over the Altar, but no flowers had been arranged on either side of the Cross, which was gold and set with impressive precious stones.

Manella became aware of an atmosphere of sanctity in the Chapel. It must have come, she thought, from the prayers of those who had worshipped there for many generations of the family.

She knelt down at the Altar rail.

She had just started saying a prayer of thankfulness to God that she was now safe for the moment when she heard voices.

She felt that they were coming closer to the Chapel and she then looked round.

She had no wish to be discovered by the Marquis or his friends. She did not want to have to explain to him her position in the household.

On one side of the Altar was a door that she guessed would lead into a Vestry.

Quickly she moved towards it and going inside found that she was right.

It was a very small Vestry, but there was a black surplice hanging on one wall and on the other there was a much more elaborate vestment.

Manella thought that it was what a Parson would traditionally wear at Christmas or some other Festival.

There was a table in the centre on which stood two Registers and several Prayer Books.

She pressed the door and it closed behind her.

As she did so, she realised that two men had now come into the Chapel and were talking in French.

She was very sure that they must be the Comte de Fiosse, whose name Mr. Dobbins had mispronounced and the other French gentleman.

"This will do nicely," one Frenchman then commented.

"I thought you would think so," the other replied. "I have told Father Anton to come in secretly and to hide here until we appear."

"There is no one likely to be looking for him," the first Frenchman replied, "and I have ascertained from his Lordship that they have a Service here for the staff only on Sundays. The Vicar from the village takes it."

"Father Anton will be here as soon as we have finished dinner," the other man said. "The only person we now have to see is the cook."

"I expect she is some fat old body who has been here since the year 'dot'," was the reply, "and for a couple of *louis* she will do anything we want!"

"Don't forget to make it sovereigns," the other told him.

"Of course I won't," was the answer. "I am not as stupid as that and I think that a 'fiver' would be about right anyway."

"You must make very sure that she understands exactly what we want."

"You can trust me," the first Frenchman replied. "I have a way with older women."

"And with young ones too!" his friend added,

They both laughed.

Without saying anything more they turned and walked straight out of the Chapel.

Manella heard their footsteps going further and further away down the long passage.

She then came out from her hiding place in the Vestry.

She found it hard to believe what she had just heard from these strange Frenchmen.

There was very obviously something very sinister taking place.

Why was a Priest necessary? And a Catholic Priest as well from the way they had spoken about him.

'I don't understand,' she told herself.

Then she remembered that one of the Frenchmen, she expected it to be the Comte, was going to see the 'cook' and he thought that she would be an elderly buxom woman.

Manella could not imagine why he would wish to see her, but it was clearly something very important.

'Of one thing I am quite certain,' she thought, 'he will have a shock when he sees me!'

It was a worrying thought.

Then she told herself that there was nothing that she could do about it.

CHAPTER FOUR

Manella had only just got back to the kitchen when one of the footmen came in to say,

"The Comte wishes to speak to you, miss. He be in the writin' room."

"And where is that?" Manella enquired.

"I'll show you right away," the footman replied.

He was a rather good-looking young man and he smiled at her before he went ahead.

They passed by the pantry and then going towards the hall there was a door on the right hand side of the corridor.

The footman opened it and Manella saw that it was a small well-furnished writing room with two desks.

One wall was covered with what seemed an avalanche of books and there were plenty of comfortable chairs and sofas scattered over the room.

Standing waiting for her was one of the Frenchmen who she had heard speaking in the Chapel.

As the footman closed the door behind him, he stared at her in amazement.

"I asked for the cook," he demanded in English.

Manella answered him in French.

"I am the cook, Monsieur le Comte."

She smiled.

"I am French by birth, but I have always lived in England."

"This is certainly a surprise," the Comte said. "I was expecting an English cook who had been with the family for years and whom I could congratulate on the excellent food she gave us for dinner last night."

"I think, being French, *monsieur,* you will enjoy the meal I am preparing for tonight," Manella told him.

"You mean you are giving us French dishes?" the Comte asked.

"*Oui, monsieur,* and I shall be extremely disappointed if you don't enjoy them," Manella answered.

"I will certainly do that," the Comte replied, "especially when I think of how charming and attractive their creator is."

Manella realised that, French fashion, he was actually flirting with her.

She merely stood waiting and hoping that he would think she was in a hurry.

"What I wanted to tell you," the Comte began, "besides, of course, complimenting you on your cooking last night, is that my friends and I have planned a little surprise for Monsieur le Marquis."

Manella inclined her head, but she did not speak.

"What we intend is to inject in him a little of the *joie de vivre*, *élan* and enthusiasm that you, *mademoiselle*, will be aware is very French."

He paused.

Then he drew a small box from the pocket of his coat.

It obviously had originally been a snuffbox. It was enamel with what Manella suspected was the Comte's crest on the lid.

He held it in his hand and looked down at it reflectively.

Then he said,

"In this box is a powdered herb, which you, being so young, *mademoiselle*, may not have heard of. It is grown in the South of France and has just reached Paris. Anyone who takes it feels an ecstasy as if they were flying up into the sky."

"It sounds very interesting," Manella said, "and you are quite right, *monsieur*, I have not heard of this herb and its properties."

"Then you will see its effect this evening," the Comte said. "What I want you to do is to put a little, a very little, into the food of Monsieur le Marquis."

He frowned for an instance and then went on,

"I don't know what your menu will be, but I am sure you can choose something, perhaps served towards the end of the meal, that will absorb quite easily just a very small teaspoonful of this magical powder."

He opened the box as he spoke and Manella could see that it was full of white powder.

"Now you do fully understand that this is only for Monsieur le Marquis," the Comte said. "On no account must any of it be wasted on me or my friends."

"I understand," Manella said.

The Comte looked round vaguely,

"Now what can I put the powder into?" he enquired.

Manella reached out and took the box from his hand.

"I will take it, *monsieur,*" she said, "and in case it gets lost or someone tastes it, I will put a teaspoonful into something safe and lock it away in a drawer in the kitchen."

"That is a good idea," the Comte said approvingly.

"It will not take me more than a minute to hurry to the kitchen and do what I suggested." Manella said.

She thought that he was going to expostulate at her suggestion.

But, before she had finished speaking, she went out of the room, closing the door behind her.

Carrying the snuffbox in her hand, she went into the kitchen and found that there was no one there.

Taking down a cup from where it hung on the dresser she emptied the whole contents of the snuffbox into it.

She next locked the cup containing the white powder safely in a drawer.

Then she re-filled the snuffbox with white flour.

It looked much the same as the powder that she had just removed from the snuffbox.

Closing the box she hurried back with it to the writing room.

The Comte was there waiting for her with a widening frown on his forehead as if he was feeling anxious.

"You have been very careful?" he said sharply as Manella entered the room. "You must give Monsieur le Marquis only half a teaspoonful or, I might well say, the contents of a small coffee-spoon."

"I understand perfectly, *monsieur*," Manella replied, "and I have only taken exactly that amount."

"You must be very sure that the footmen serve what is for Monsieur le Marquis to him and not to any of us. It would be a disaster if the plate went to the wrong person."

"I appreciate that," Manella answered, "and I do promise you, *monsieur,* that there will be no mistakes."

"I know that I can trust you," the Comte said putting the snuffbox into his pocket without opening it, "and here is something for your trouble so that you can buy a gown to make you look even lovelier than you are at the moment."

He pressed five sovereigns into her hand and she dropped him a curtsey.

"*Merci beaucoup, Monsieur le Comte*," she said, "You are indeed most kind and I am very grateful."

"It would, you understand, be a great mistake," the Comte said softly, "for anyone in the house to know of my generosity."

"Of course, *monsieur*," Manella agreed.

She walked to the door and curtseyed again before she left him.

She went back to the kitchen and then she opened the drawer and looked speculatively at the contents of the cup.

She had an idea in her head and, the more she thought about it, the better it became.

Manella started to prepare the dinner earlier than would have been necessary.

But with the Comte's interference there was now a new addition to what she had already planned.

When she told Mr. Dobbins that they were having a French menu, he had commented,

"That's somethin' new for all of us, but his Lordship may have acquired different tastes bein' so long out in France."

"That is what I thought, Mr. Dobbins," Manella smiled, "and I want your help to see that everything goes off smoothly."

"I'm only here to oblige," Mr. Dobbins said jokingly.

Manella made out the menu and took it along to Mr. Wilson.

"French dishes?" he enquired. "You would have thought that his Lordship would be tired of them by now."

"One can never tire of a good thing," Manella replied, "and French food, I assure you, Mr. Wilson, is very very good."

"Well, there were no complaints about last night's dinner," Mr. Wilson said. "And I'll not pretend, Miss Chinon, that you were not a 'gift from the Gods' when we most needed it."

"*Merci beaucoup, monsieur*," Manella replied, "and I rather like being a Goddess!"

She heard him laugh as she left the room to hurry back to the kitchen.

She had chosen a dinner that she had cooked many times for her beloved father.

There was a very delicious duck pâté to start with and she served it on individual plates decorated with rosettes made from baby carrots and small beetroots.

After that came a cup filled with clear golden soup.

Every mouthful of which, Manella well knew, was a sheer delight.

This was followed by a fresh salmon, which the estate gamekeeper had brought in that very morning from the river.

At the same time they had provided her with four young chickens.

'*Petits poussins*', as Manella had described them on the menu.

She had then hesitated to think and decided to add between the salmon and the *poussins* a pear *sorbet*.

She added just a touch of champagne and it was to be served in wine glasses.

Then she thought with a little twinkle in her eyes that this would be something different from what they had eaten last night.

She concentrated now on the *poussins*.

*

Dinner was announced ceremoniously by Dobbins at exactly eight o'clock.

It was late by London standards because the Prince Regent usually liked to dine at seven-thirty.

But, while the weather was so fine, the Marquis wanted to be out in the grounds as late as he possibly could be.

He had been riding during the afternoon a horse that he had purchased at Tattersalls two weeks ago for what he considered to be a rather extravagant price.

It was not completely broken in, so he enjoyed the age-old battle between man and beast that every generation of his family had always greatly appreciated.

They sat down at the table decorated with orchids.

The Comtesse put her hand with its long thin fingers on his arm and said,

"Dearest Buck, it is delightful to have you to ourselves. I shall be jealous tomorrow when the rest of your party arrives."

"I would hope that you are not suggesting in a subtle way that I may neglect you," the Marquis replied.

"I would never allow you to do so," the Comtesse then insisted with an innuendo behind every word.

The Marquis had met her in Paris at a luncheon party and found her witty, amusing and completely insatiable in bed.

After the demands and strains of the War he had found that Paris, with an elasticity all of its own, had come back to life.

There was every possible amusement for a man who wished to be amused.

It enabled him to forget the carnage, the suffering and the deprivations of so many years.

Yvette had made sure that the Marquis thought more of her than of anything or anyone else.

She was always there when he was not actually on duty with his troops and he would have been inhuman if he had not found that she was extremely desirable.

She had made sure, as only a sophisticated woman could, that he was passionate about her.

She was a widow.

Her husband had been killed in action when he was commanding his Regiment at the Battle of Leipzig, the year before Napoleon's abdication and banishment to Elba.

Yvette had impressed upon the Marquis over and over again that she came from a family of the *Ancien Régime*.

But her husband had had no choice but to fight for the 'Corsican Corporal', once he had seized power.

"If Henri was alive," she said, "he would have been so glad that the English won and that you, *mon brave*, had been recognised as a great soldier."

Her brother, the Comte, duly confirmed everything she said.

He reiterated over and over again how, although they had luckily escaped the guillotine, their estates were all taken from them during the Revolution.

"The rightful place for aristocrats now is England," he said, "and that is where dearest Yvette wishes to live."

When he said this, he gave the Marquis a look that expressed better than words what he was hoping would happen.

The Marquis, however, had been pursued since leaving Eton and Cambridge University by women who wished to marry him because of his title and huge estates.

And for the wealth and power he would inherit when his father died.

When he did become the Earl, he was then fighting in Portugal and more concerned with keeping alive than with his possessions at home.

He had however not failed to notice that after he became the Marquis of Buckingdon the invitation cards that appeared on his breakfast table every morning had increased remarkably in number.

It seemed extraordinary for a man who had so much that he could admit to himself that he had never been in love.

He had been intrigued by female wiles and at times infatuated.

But he had never been in love to the critical point where he wished to share the rest of his life with any woman.

Yvette had made it only too obvious in Paris that she really wanted to become an English Countess. And now, all the more, to become the Marchioness of Buckingdon.

He thought that she was now being rather too persistent and possessive.

He told himself that, when he returned to London, he would not see so much of her.

He had talked, and what man would not, when he was abroad of the house he loved and his horses that meant so much to him.

He had therefore thought it would be polite, if nothing else, to bring Yvette, her brother and the Frenchman who was nearly always with them to visit Buckingdon Castle.

Now he decided that this would be most definitely both the first and the last visit that they would make.

He was grateful to them, of course he was grateful, for all they had done for him in Paris.

But now that he was back in England, he knew that he must concentrate on his family and make contact with the friends he had known when he was a boy.

Moreover what was known as the *Beau Monde* was waiting for his return to London.

The Prince Regent had made it very clear that he would be a welcome guest at any time that he wished to visit Carlton House.

Last night Yvette had been even more demanding than usual.

The Marquis had actually been somewhat tired after the long drive down from London.

He decided that he would buy her a present of emeralds that matched her eyes and that would be that.

"At least," Yvette was saying now in a soft seductive voice, "we shall have a little time to ourselves tomorrow before your party arrives."

"Of course we shall," the Marquis answered, "and you must tell me what you would like to do. There are still a lot of things I have not shown you and my horses are waiting for your orders."

Yvette smiled at him provocatively.

He knew that what she wanted did not include horses. But he was now well aware that she really did not fit into the English countryside.

He would have actually been much wiser to give a party for her at his house in Berkeley Square.

Dobbins and the footmen were now placing the *pâté* in front of the guests.

The Marquis reached out his hand for the menu.

It was in a gold holder that bore his ancestral Coat of Arms.

He read it and then turned to Yvette,

"I see we have a French dinner tonight and that, of course, is in your honour. I only hope that as my cook is English you will not be disappointed."

"How could I be possibly disappointed in anything in this wonderful Castle of yours," Yvette gushed, "and, as you know well, Buck, it is made for love."

The Marquis tasted the *pâté* and, instead of replying to Yvette, he said,

"This is excellent! I had no idea that Mrs. Wade could make a *pâté* as good as this!"

"I would like to say we had brought it with us," the Comte interposed, "but unfortunately I did not think of it."

"If you had, it would have been 'coals to Newcastle'!" the Marquis replied. "Do you not agree with me, Grave?"

The other Frenchman nodded enthusiastically.

Salmon cooked in its juices followed the soup. By this time they were all exclaiming that they had never tasted better dishes so beautifully cooked.

The *sorbet* was a surprise and then Dobbins went to the Marquis's side.

"Cook asks me to tell you, my Lord," he said, "that it's usual in this part of the country, when a man returns from war for him to be given the 'White Dove of Peace' as a very special dish."

He took a deep breath and then went on,

"'Tis supposed to bring him luck so's he'll not have to fight again. Cook asks that you eats it all yourself as is traditional and not share it with anyone else!'"

The Marquis listened and then he laughed.

"This is a legend that I have never heard of before," he said. "Of course I will do what cook asks, but I see that the 'White Dove of Peace' is not on the menu."

"No, my Lord," Dobbins replied, "but there are 'baby poussins', I think she calls 'em' for everyone else."

The Marquis's eyes twinkled, but he did not correct Dobbins's mispronunciation.

A footman put the delightfully cooked *poussins* in front of the other guests.

They were served a special stuffing and gravy containing fresh mushrooms as well as the usual breadcrumbs.

On a side plate there were tiny carrots, all no bigger than marbles, baby beetroot of about the same size and minute green peas.

There were new potatoes cooked 'in their jackets' that were merely a mouthful each.

The Marquis then tasted his 'White Dove of Peace'.

He thought secretly that it was a delicious and very well-cooked pigeon and he certainly could not find fault with it.

In fact it was tenderer than any pigeon that he had ever eaten before.

There was a long silence while everyone ate.

Then suddenly Monsieur Grave, who was sitting opposite the Marquis, made a murmur.

He put out his hands as if to support himself and then fell forward, his face falling into his plate.

The Marquis stared at him in astonishment and thinking that the fellow must be drunk.

Then before he could say or do anything, Yvette fell backwards in her chair.

Collapsing, she slipped down under the table.

The Marquis pushed back his chair as next the Comte, with a crash fell forward, his hand upsetting his glass of champagne as he did so.

Standing up the Marquis stared at his guests for the moment speechless.

Then, as Dobbins came running to his side, he asserted,

"What the devil does this mean? Go fetch the cook! It must be something to do with the food."

Dobbins moved over the room to obey him while the footmen stood waiting for orders.

They were just staring at the guests as the Marquis was doing.

Manella was in fact waiting just outside the dining room.

She had been afraid that the Marquis might eat one of the *poussins* rather than the pigeon that she had prepared specially for him.

She had peered into the room so that she could save him if it was necessary.

She had put all the powder that had been in the snuffbox into the stuffing of the *poussins* and into the gravy.

Dobbins had no need to speak to her.

As he reached the door, she walked past him and then up to where the Marquis was still standing at the head of the table.

As she faced him, he looked at her in astonishment and exclaimed,

"You are not Mrs. Wade!"

"Mrs. Wade has been suddenly taken ill and I have replaced her," Manella said quietly.

"Then you are responsible for this?" the Marquis asked, indicating his collapsed guests.

"They have consumed a drug that was intended for you, my Lord," Manella told him.

"For me?"

"Monsieur le Comte gave me five gold sovereigns to put half a teaspoonful of what is obviously a drug into your food and into no one else's. But instead I put a very large quantity of the drug into their food." Manella explained.

"I cannot believe it!" the Marquis exclaimed, "Whyever should he do that?"

"I think you will find the explanation in the Chapel," Manella replied.

The Marquis looked at her and she realised that he did not understand.

"I had overheard them saying that a Priest, and I should imagine a Roman Catholic one, would be waiting there after dinner."

She saw from the expression in the Marquis's eyes that at last he understood and it made him very angry.

There was a hard look in his eyes and his lips tightened into a straight line.

Then he said in a very controlled voice,

"So obviously I must thank you for saving me."

"Any of your *English* admirers, and there are most certainly a great many of them, my Lord, would have done the same."

She emphasised the word 'English' and knew that the Marquis would take it as a rebuke.

He was looking thoughtful for a moment.

Then he said,

"We will discuss this later. In the meantime I will get rid of this rabble."

Manella knew that she was dismissed.

She dropped the Marquis a small curtsey.

Only when she reached the door did she hear him giving sharp orders to Dobbins as if he was on a battlefield.

She then tidied up the kitchen and looked sadly at the raspberry *soufflé* she had prepared just in case it was needed.

The *poussins*, however, had done their work very competently.

Manella had read about drugs of various sorts in books in her father's library.

She was intelligent enough to recognise that the Comte had intended to give the Marquis just enough to sap his willpower.

They would then have taken him from the dining room to the Chapel.

There he would have acquiesced without any demur to Yvette's demand to be his wife.

They would have been married by the Priest who was waiting for them in the Chapel.

Then there would have been no possible escape for him.

'But I saved him!' Manella thought triumphantly. 'Now perhaps he will realise that the French are not to be trusted either in war or in peace.'

She was aware that she was being disloyal to her grandmother.

At the same time Napoleon had altered the whole social make-up of France and it was a very different country now from all that it had been in the past.

The staff had all had their dinner earlier, in fact at six o'clock, which was the usual time for them.

Manella therefore had nothing to do now except wait for the Marquis to summon her.

She sat down at the kitchen table and started to read a book.

It was over three-quarters-of-an-hour later that Dobbins came into the kitchen.

"'His Lordship wishes to see you in his study, Miss Chinon," he said, "and you've never heard such goin's on!"

"What has happened?" Manella asked him.

"His Lordship's had the phaeton that Monsieur Grave came in brought round to the front of the house. They was all three pushed into it. Sound asleep, they all was! Couldn't get a peep out of any of them. All their luggage was thrown up behind and the groom was told to take the lot back to London or as far as he could get!"

Mr. Dobbins gave a laugh.

"He wasn't at all pleased, settin' off at night with them all squeezed in like sardines at the back of the phaeton."

"They had not – recovered – consciousness?" Manella asked a little tentatively.

She had really no wish to kill anyone, even scoundrels.

"They had no idea of what was happening to 'em. But they was alive all right, the Comte snorin' as if he were a bear at the zoo!"

"I expect they will have a huge headache tomorrow," Manella commented.

"That's just what I thinks too," Mr. Dobbins replied, "and it serves them right! How dare they try to drug his Lordship? I've told you before and I'll tell you again, you can never trust them 'Frogs'."

He suddenly realised who he was speaking to.

"But then you're different, miss," he said, "as we all knows. You seems to me to be more English than French and that be the truth."

"I will take that as a compliment, Mr. Dobbins, and I am indeed grateful," Manella said. "Now I must go to his Lordship."

She walked out of the kitchen and down the long corridor that led to the study.

She knew where it was.

When she had reached the hall, one of the footmen went ahead and then opened the door for her.

Once inside she saw that it was a very attractive room.

Hie pictures were all of horses, set against soft green walls which had been one of Robert Adams's favourite colours.

The Marquis was standing in front of the fireplace which, because it was summer, was filled with flowering plants.

His eyes were on Manella as she walked towards him.

When she reached him, she made a small but graceful curtsey.

"Do sit down, Mademoiselle Chinon, which I am told is your name," he said, "and I hear too that you are French."

"I told Mr. Dobbins that my parents were French *émigrés* just before the Revolution." Manella replied. "But my father's father was English although his wife, my grandmother, was French. So my father was half-French and I am only a quarter French."

The Marquis laughed and it broke the tension.

"But you certainly cook like a Frenchwoman," he said, "and I enjoyed every mouthful of the five courses that were served to me."

He drew in his breath.

"Why did you not warn me what they were plotting against me?"

"I had no idea what the result of the drug would in fact be," Manella replied. "The Comte merely told me it would give you a *joie de vivre* and a sense of joy and delight that is often sadly missing in the English."

"What he did not say was that it would sap my willpower," the Marquis said, "and you have already told me why they wanted to do that."

"What have you – done about the – Priest?" Manella asked him curiously.

"I told him that if he is ever seen to set foot on my land again I will have him arrested for conspiracy," the Marquis replied. " I have never seen a man run faster!"

Manella laughed.

"I have already – heard how you have rid yourself of those – friends."

"And that leaves you," the Marquis said, "to whom I am exceedingly grateful. Tell me, Miss Chinon, how I can thank you for all you have done for me."

"I am actually thanking you," Manella answered, "because I was fortunate enough when I was looking for work to hear that Mrs. Wade, your cook, had been taken very ill. And I was allowed to bring with me my horse and, as you can see, my dog."

Flash had been at her heels when she left the kitchen and had come along with her into the study.

He was now lying quietly at her feet.

"If your horse is as good-looking as your dog," the Marquis said, "I shall be interested to see him."

"I love Heron, as I love Flash," Manella said, "and I was so very very thankful that we could stay here where – no one will – find us."

She spoke without thinking and the Marquis insisted quickly,

"So you *are* running away! I thought that might be the reason why I had the pleasure of your company!"

"Yes – I am running – away," Manella admitted, "but – I do *not* wish to – talk about it."

"Then we will talk about something else," the Marquis said. "Tell me what do you think of my Castle."

"You must know the answer to that," Manella replied. "It is magnificent and exactly the right background for you."

"Now you are complimenting me," the Marquis remarked with a twinkle in his eyes.

"How could I do anything else when you have fought so gallantly under the great Duke of Wellington and have been rewarded for your bravery?" Manella asked.

"By becoming a Marquis?" he asked. "I think really I am prouder of being the eleventh Earl."

"The next step is a Dukedom, if you want to go higher," Manella pointed out with a grin.

"That is something I certainly have no wish to do," the Marquis answered. "I have had enough of fighting. I want to sleep in my own bed in my own house and ride over my own land."

"Then that is exactly what you are now able to do," Manella smiled.

There was a pause and then she realised that the Marquis was looking at her in a way that made her feel shy and rather uncomfortable.

Unexpectedly he said,

"I want to see your horse and I feel sure that he is as exceptional as his Mistress and her dog. Will you ride with me tomorrow morning?"

"I would love to do that," Manella replied. "I was thinking earlier today that, as you rode so early, I should have to get up even earlier to exercise him so that I would not be in your way."

"You will not be that," the Marquis said, "when we ride together."

There was a little pause and they both looked at each other.

Manella had the strange feeling that they were speaking without words.

Then the Marquis said somewhat abruptly,

"I have sent grooms to tell my friends who were coming tomorrow that I unfortunately cannot be here after all to receive them."

"You did that?" Manella exclaimed, "But why?"

"Because," the Marquis said, "however careful we may be, what has happened tonight is too good a story not to be repeated over and over again by anyone who hears it and the Press will soon pick it up for lurid publishing."

"Yes, of course. I had not thought – of that," Manella murmured.

"I doubt very much if those French people I have just turned out will talk, but you cannot prevent servants from doing so. Any guests who come to stay tonight will bring their valets, their lady's maids and grooms. The story will be carried back to London. That is inevitable," the Marquis reflected thoughtfully.

"You are very wise," Manella said. "It would certainly be a – mistake for people to – talk about what has – occurred."

She thought with a little shiver that in some way even her uncle might get to hear of it.

If he was told that the pretty cook who had saved the Marquis's life had a horse and a dog, it would not take him long 'to put two and two together'.

She shivered again and the Marquis exclaimed,

"You are frightened! Who has frightened you and why, tell me?"

Manella made a little gesture with her hands.

"As I have already told your Lordship, I do not want to talk about it."

"I might well be able to help you," the Marquis said. "I am usually very good at sorting out problems and I certainly had plenty of them during the War. Why not trust me and see if I can manage to wipe away that sign of fear in your eyes?"

She realised that he was being very kind and she looked up at him gratefully before she replied,

"I think – for the moment – I am safe, but – if I am not – I will come and tell you."

"Is that a promise?" the Marquis asked.

"It is a promise!" Manella assured him.

She had the strange feeling that, having promised him what he asked for, she would find it impossible not to turn to him if she really was in trouble.

CHAPTER FIVE

Manella found it difficult to sleep.

It was not really surprising seeing how much had happened during the evening.

She kept thinking about it all and about the Marquis as well.

He had been so kind and understanding.

When she had risen to say 'goodnight', the Marquis had queried,

"What about our early morning ride? Shall we say seven o'clock? Or is that too early for you?"

"It is not too early," Manella answered, "but I ought to be preparing your breakfast."

The Marquis laughed.

"If I have to wait a few minutes after we arrive back," he said, "I will, of course, forgive you."

Manella walked to the door, but the Marquis reached it first.

"I cannot let you go without thanking you again for saving me," he said, "from a danger that I had not anticipated even in my wildest dreams."

"How could you have imagined for s single moment that anyone would do anything so – wicked?" Manella enquired.

"I have always prided myself," he said, "on being a step ahead of the enemy and using my perception. This evening I failed lamentably on both those counts, so I can only thank you once again and tell you how very very grateful I am."

As he spoke, he took her hand and lifted it to his lips.

Manella thought that he would just bend over it as a Frenchman would have done.

Instead his lips actually touched her skin.

It gave her a strange feeling that ran through her body like a streak of lightning.

Then, because she was shy, she moved away from him.

When she was outside the study, she ran towards the hall.

There was only one sleepy footman on duty, sitting in the usual padded chair, but he did not move when he saw her.

Manella ran up the stairs with Flash following her and reached her bedroom.

When she did so, she felt now almost free from the terror that she had felt when she was running away from her uncle.

She walked over to the window and pulled back the curtains.

The moon was shining on the lake and the stars glittered brightly overhead.

And she could not explain to herself in any way why she should suddenly feel wildly and ecstatically excited.

*

Manella reached the stables at five minutes to seven.

She was really not in the least surprised to find that the Marquis was already there.

He was carefully choosing which one of his many horses he would wish to ride and he had already given orders for Heron to be saddled for her.

When, a few minutes later, they set off going out through the back of the stables, he said,

"I admire your taste in horses as much as I admire your cooking!"

"Heron appreciates your compliment, my Lord," she replied, "when you have so many fine horses of your own."

"I intend to have a great many more," the Marquis said. "My last charger in France will also be coming home to spend his declining years peacefully and in comfort."

Manella thought it was just like him and what she had expected that he would love the horses which had served him.

He would make sure that they ended their days in happiness and comfort.

She knew that it was something that her uncle would never even think about.

The horses she had left behind at home would be sold or destroyed as soon as her uncle could afford to replace them.

"You are not looking happy," the Marquis commented unexpectedly. "Why?"

Manella forced herself to smile.

"I was just thinking of how many poor horses, after they have served their Masters well, are sold to the butcher or just left to starve to death."

"We cannot change the world overnight," the Marquis said, "but at least we can try, each in our own small way."

It was the sort of thing, Manella thought, that he would say.

She smiled at him before he suggested,

"I will race you, or rather Tempest, which is the name of the horse I am now riding and we will challenge Heron."

They had reached some level ground.

Although Manella tried in every way she could think of to beat him, the Marquis was half a length ahead of her by the time they reached the end.

"You – won!" she managed to call out to him breathlessly.

"And you are the very best rider of any woman I have ever seen!" the Marquis answered. "Don't tell me it is because you are French, when I well know that it is entirely due to your English blood!"

Manella laughed.

"That I will accept, my Lord, and thank you so much for the compliment."

"I am merely stating a fact," the Marquis went on, "and, of course, I am curious to know why you are having to earn your living when you possess so fine a horse as Heron."

"I have already told you, it is a secret," Manella said. "I happened to arrive in the village at exactly the right moment as far as I was concerned, when your cook had had a stroke and your butler was frantic in case you should go hungry."

The Marquis laughed.

"I am quite certain that Dobbins thought he was dreaming when you told him that you could cook."

He paused, looked at her, and then added,

"And, of course, I am dreaming as well. It is impossible that anyone could look like you, cook like you, ride like you and yet be a human being!"

"I shall become conceited if you say such nice things to me," Manella said, "and I know that Tempest and Heron want to show you how well they can jump."

The Marquis rode ahead of her to where there were a number of low fences separating two large fields.

Both horses sailed over them gracefully without any apparent effort and then he said,

"There is a Racecourse on my land, which I know has deteriorated, but I will certainly have it restored for use. Then we will just see if Heron can outjump Tempest, which I have a strong suspicion that he will be able to do."

"It will be very exciting for him and I shall be praying hard that he succeeds." Manella said enthusiastically.

"It would be a most unfair handicap for Tempest," the Marquis remarked.

They laughed a great deal more before they turned their mounts and started to return to The Castle.

Only as they were within sight of the stables did the Marquis say,

"It is difficult to tell you exactly how much I have enjoyed our ride, Manella. What are you going to do for the rest of the day?"

"I have not yet given it much thought," Manella replied. "Will you be alone now that you have put off the visit of your friends?"

"I was hoping that I could spend it with you," the Marquis said, "and I have a suggestion to make that I hope you will agree to."

Manella looked at him from under her eyelashes.

"Is that an order or a request, my Lord?"

"I always like to have things my own way," the Marquis replied at once.

He then told her that there was a very interesting view from a special place on his estate.

It was reputed that from it one could, with the help of a telescope or binoculars, see five different Counties.

"I thought it would be amusing to take you there," he added. "We should either leave before luncheon or else take it with us if you would be so obliging as to get it ready."

Manella's eyes were shining at the idea,

Then she asked a little hesitantly,

"You – don't think the – household will be – shocked at you – going driving with your – cook?"

"If they are, I must just put up with it," the Marquis answered. "But I have a feeling that Dobbins and Mrs. Franklin, who was my Nanny when I was a small boy, will understand that now I have returned home I would wish to share my enthusiasm for my estate with someone and why not you?"

"That is very plausible," Manella responded teasingly, "but your Lordship knows as well as I do that – servants talk."

"They will talk anyway, as will the village, at my having such a pretty and clever cook," the Marquis said, "who also has French blood in her veins."

"That is supposedly a handicap," Manella suggested.

"As I would hope to eat some more of your French dishes tonight," the Marquis said, "it is definitely, as far as I am concerned, a splendid asset!"

When they reached the stables, Manella thanked him politely and then hurried back into The Castle through the kitchen door.

She found to her relief that Bessie and Jane had already prepared some of the dishes for dinner.

She put her riding hat and her jacket onto a chair. Quickly she cooked the dishes and actually had three ready when Dobbins came in to say that his Lordship was already in the dining room.

"Ask him to start with these, Mr. Dobbins," Manella said, "and I will have the fish and the kidneys ready by the time he has finished."

Dobbins did not say anything.

She had the feeling that he was thinking that his world had turned upside down and he would never again be surprised at anything.

Everyone had so much to say about what had happened the previous night.

They hardly seemed to notice when Manella sent a large hamper from the kitchen to the stables.

There was another smaller one containing wine, water and coffee.

She had gone up to her room after breakfast to change from her riding habit into one of the pretty light gowns that Heron had carried on his saddle.

The only outstanding problem was that, while she had brought three gowns with her, she had not included any hats to go with them.

She was wondering what she could do when Mrs. Franklin came into the room.

"I hear his Lordship's inspectin' the estate," she said, "and that you're goin' with him to give him his luncheon."

"That is what he has asked me to do," Manella answered.

"And quite right too!" Mrs. Franklin said to Manella's surprise. "The food they serves at the inns round here isn't somethin' I'd set before his Lordship. I'm certain you've arranged a good meal for him."

"I have certainly tried to do so," Manella agreed.

"Well, all I can say," Mrs. Franklin went on, "is that those who tried to trap his Lordship last night shouldn't have been allowed to sample the good food you gave them to start with! Sheer waste, that's what I calls it, on rats like them!"

"I agree with you," Manella said, "but please remember that his Lordship enjoyed all five courses and that is all that matters."

"You are so right!" Mrs. Franklin said. "Anyway, if you're goin' now with his Lordship, you'll see some of the land that's been in the family for six generations."

She talked possessively and Manella understood that she and Dobbins definitely thought of themselves as part of the family.

"I have told Bessie and Jane what to do for your luncheon, Mrs. Franklin," Manella said, "and, although it will be cold, I hope you will enjoy it."

"Now, don't you go worryin' about us," Mrs. Franklin said. "You just have a good time while you are young. Troubles come with old age and regrets."

She spoke wistfully and Manella wondered if she had been unhappy with Mr. Franklin if such a person had actually existed.

She knew that it was usual for housekeepers and cooks to be called 'Mrs.' whether they were married or not.

She made no comment, but said instead,

"Mrs. Franklin, I have no hat to wear as I rode here."

"I never thought of that," Mrs. Franklin answered. "I'm sure I could find you one later in her late Ladyship's trunks that are all packed away upstairs in the attics. All I can suggest for the moment is that you take a sunshade."

"That is a very good idea!" Manella replied. "I knew you would help me."

"I'll get the hats down just in case you want one another time," Mrs. Franklin promised, "but the sunshades are here at the end of the passage."

She went out of the room to where on the other side of the corridor there were a number of doors.

Manella was already aware that it was where most of The Castle's linen was kept and all the State Rooms were edged with handmade lace.

Mrs. Franklin then opened one of the doors and came back with two small sunshades in her hands. They were just right for carrying when one was in a phaeton.

Not too big to blow away, but large enough to keep off the sun,

Manella chose one of a pale pink with a frill round the edge.

It went very well with her gown, she thought, which was of muslin and embroidered with small field flowers.

"Of one thing I'm quite certain," Mrs. Franklin said, "you'll not see many people in this part of the world. But if you do, carry your sunshade close over your head and it won't show that you're not wearin' a hat."

"I will do so," Manella smiled, "and thank you so much for your advice, Mrs. Franklin."

She ran down the stairs on winged feet.

When she reached the hall, she could through the open front door that the Marquis was outside.

He was patting the fine horses that drew his phaeton while two footmen were putting the hampers into the back of it.

The Marquis, seeing Manella approach, said,

"Let me help you into the phaeton, Miss Chinon. I hope that you will not be frightened if I drive fast."

"I will try not to be, my Lord," Manella answered demurely.

He helped her onto the high seat, then climbed up himself and picked up the reins.

The groom was on the single rather precarious seat just behind them.

Then they drove off and Manella opened her parasol and held it elegantly over her head.

"What has happened to your hat?" the Marquis enquired.

"I could not think when I was running away how Heron could carry it," she replied.

He drove on a little way, tooling his horses with what Manella knew was an expert hand.

"Are you going to tell me who you are running away from?" the Marquis asked finally "and why?"

Manella turned to look at him.

"Please – allow me to forget everything today – and just enjoy myself," she pleaded. "I do not want to – think about why I have come to The Castle –

or what happened last night. I just want to enjoy these – fabulous horses that are pulling us – and think of how many women would gnash their teeth if they knew that – I was driving alone with the Hero of Waterloo!"

The Marquis's eyes twinkled.

"Very elusive," he remarked, "and clever enough to make sure that I can no longer go on fighting to win your confidence."

"Is that what you want to do?" Manella quizzed him.

"On the contrary," he replied, "this is the sheer peace I have always wanted, driving over my own land behind my own horses and, of course, beside the most beautiful young woman I have ever met!"

Because there was a distinct note of sincerity in his voice, Manella blushed.

They drove on for a long way almost in silence.

Finally the Marquis brought the horses to a standstill in the centre of a wood.

To Manella's surprise she saw that there was a little wooden house nestling under some tall lime trees.

She looked at the Marquis for an explanation and he told her,

"This is where we have shooting luncheons and I do think we will find it more enjoyable than sitting on the grass or propping our backs up against the trunk of a tree."

"Of course," Manella agreed, "and it is so pretty."

The Marquis told the groom to carry in the hampers and Manella began to unpack them.

To start the meal there was some of the excellent *pâté* left over from last night.

After that there were wafer-thin slices of every cold meat that Manella could find in the larder.

She had not forgotten to put in a most delicious French sauce as well as a salad prepared in the French manner.

The Marquis declared that it was all really delicious.

After that there were several varieties of cheese including a cream cheese that she had made herself the previous day.

Then there were *croissants* that she had cooked the night before and they spread them with thick Jersey butter, which came from one of the Marquis's farms.

The Marquis enjoyed everything he ate and there was champagne and a white wine to drink with the meal.

Manella then poured out the coffee from a flask.

They sat talking for a long time at an ancient oak table inside the little house.

The windows were all open and sparkling sunshine poured in.

There was the song of the birds outside and the sound of small animals scuttling about in the undergrowth.

The groom had gone deeper into the wood where there was a pool of spring water for the horses to drink.

Manella felt as if she and the Marquis were sitting on some strange planet in outer space and a long long way from all the worries and difficulties of her life.

The Earth, as they knew it, could not encroach on them in any way.

There was silence between them for some minutes.

Then the Marquis asked her,

"What are you thinking about now?"

"I am thinking about you," she answered. "It is impossible for me to think of anything else."

"And I am just wondering how you can be so lovely and at the same time so clever. I am well aware that this picnic you have brought is very different from the picnic that Mrs. Wade would have packed for me. Yet you talk as if you have travelled all over the world."

"Which, of course, I have in my imagination as well as through libraries like yours," she replied.

"And I suppose that one day some man will be lucky enough to take you to all the places that you have read about and which have become such a part of your dreams?"

It was really a question that he was obviously waiting for an answer for.

Manella looked away from him before she replied,

"Of course that is what I – really hope will happen – but so far I have – not met the – gentleman in question."

She knew as soon as she spoke that the Marquis had tricked her into revealing if she had run away from a man.

She told herself that she had been foolish not to realise that was what he was doing until it was too late.

She then stood up from the table.

"If we have much further to go to see the view you have promised me," she said, "I must now start packing up the luncheon things."

She thought that the Marquis was going to expostulate. Instead he helped her put the dishes back into the basket and cork up what was left of the wine.

He then called to the groom to put the hampers back into the phaeton and then they set off once again.

It was rather doubtful if they did actually see five Counties, but the view from the top of the high mound was certainly very impressive.

When they climbed down to where the horses were waiting for them, Manella said,

"I thought when you were standing there, my Lord that you certainly are the 'Monarch of all you survey'! I am not surprised that you are proud of The Castle and the long history that lies behind it."

"Of course I am exceedingly proud of my legacy from many generations of my family," the Marquis answered. "Equally it does have its penalties."

Manella thought for a moment that he was going to tell her what those were.

Instead he now seemed to be in a hurry to go back to The Castle.

He certainly drove there very rapidly.

In fact it was so quickly that it was impossible for Manella to hold up her sunshade or even to talk more than a few words with the Marquis.

When they arrived back, the Marquis drew up his team with a flourish outside the front door.

The grooms, who were waiting for them, came hurrying to the horses' heads. He seemed to have a large number of orders to give to them.

Manella therefore went into The Castle without saying anything more to him.

As she walked slowly up the stairs, she was thinking about what an exciting day it had been.

At the same time she was puzzled at the Marquis's behaviour on the homeward journey.

Flash had been sitting very quietly at her feet in the front of the phaeton and now he was frisking about the room as if he wanted to take some exercise.

Manella put her arms round him.

"I have work to do, Flash," she said, "and, although I would like to take you for a walk, you will have to wait until after dinner."

She found herself wondering if the Marquis would send for her as he had last night.

She wanted to talk to him and she wanted to be with him.

If he was lonely, as he would be, having put off his friends, he might find her company better than having nobody to talk to at all.

'He is indeed a wonderful man,' Manella murmured to herself, 'and I am very lucky to have met him and talked to him."

Then she became alarmed because she knew that if she had to leave the Marquis, or he returned to London, she would miss him enormously.

That was something that she had never expected to feel under any circumstances.

CHAPTER SIX

Manella walked slowly up the staircase to her bedroom.

She was feeling depressed.

Since their return to The Castle after such an enjoyable ride the Marquis had not sent for her.

Nor had he made any suggestions about their riding again together tomorrow morning.

She wondered what she had done or said to have upset him.

Or was it perhaps because he had found her boring?

In the bedroom Flash turned round half-a-dozen times, as Setters do, before he settled in his usual place by the bed.

Manella undressed, feeling that somehow as if the sunshine and the moonlight were no longer with her.

She felt as if she was enveloped in a fog that she did not quite grasp.

'It was so wonderful this morning,' she said to herself again and again.

She remembered how she and the Marquis had raced their horses.

Then, when they had driven away from The Castle in his phaeton, she had thought that it was the most exciting thing she had ever done.

But she now realised just how attractive and alluring the Comtesse had been.

Perhaps the Marquis was missing her.

After the Comtesse he would undoubtedly find her dull and uninteresting.

The Comtesse had been a sophisticated and witty Frenchwoman.

Manella remembered how Dobbins had said that she had made the Marquis laugh at the things she said.

"*You knows what them 'Froggies' is like,*" he had gone on. "*I've always heard they has a double meanin' to everythin' that they says, but his Lordship seemed to understand what was meant right enough! Kept the three men in stitches, she did!*"

'Then I suppose I should try to be like that,' Manella thought wistfully.

At the same time, whatever the Marquis had thought of the Comtesse in the past, he was now disillusioned with her.

She wondered how he could ever have been so deceived by this Frenchwoman.

She had looked at the Comte and Monsieur Grave lying on the dining room table,

They appeared ugly and unpleasant especially Monsieur Grave.

She could not help thinking that no one with any sense would have trusted Monsieur Grave as a friend or an accomplice.

She had saved the Marquis, for if she had not done so, he would now be married to the Comtesse and not be able to do anything about it whether he wanted to or not.

She was trying to cheer herself up on that score, but then she thought,

'Perhaps alone in his bedroom he is regretting it and is wishing that he had her with him still.'

She brushed her hair for some time as her mother had always taught her to do.

Then she climbed into bed and blew out the candies.

In the darkness, because she felt she needed reassuring, she bent over and patted Flash's head.

"You are such a beautiful boy," she said. "I love you very much – and I know that you would never disappoint me."

She closed her eyes and started, as she always did, to say her prayers.

She was almost dropping off to sleep when she heard Flash give a low growl.

It was the sound that he invariably made when he sensed danger.

Manella wondered what it was that was worrying him so much.

He growled again and getting to his feet walked across to the window.

"What is it, Flash?" Manella whispered.

She knew instinctively that there was something wrong,

Although Flash was not barking, he was now making the sound in his throat that he made when he was annoyed.

"What is the matter?" she asked him again.

She jumped out of bed and, walking to where he was standing, drew back the curtain.

The moonlight flooded in over her in a silver stream.

Flash rose up to put his front paws on the window ledge.

Manella looked out of the window and then down to the ground.

Suddenly she was very still.

Just below her she could see quite clearly that there was a man.

He had started to climb up the outside of the house.

It was not a very difficult thing to do as the bricks were old and so many crevices gave a good foothold. Also there were the ledges of the windows on the ground floor as well as the ornamentation above them.

She stared down wondering what he could be doing.

It was then that she saw half-hidden in the bushes on the curve of the courtyard there was a closed carriage.

Beside it and just visible in the shadows were two other men.

The first man was slowly climbing up higher and higher.

And suddenly it dawned on Manella that he was now approaching her window.

It then occurred to her that he greatly resembled Monsieur Grave.

With a little cry of horror she ran across the room and pulled open the door.

She ran wildly to the only person she knew who was sleeping on this floor.

The Master Suite, which was occupied by the Marquis, was a long way from her room. But, with Flash running beside her, she reached it in only a few seconds,

She pulled open the door at once and, without hesitating for a minute, passed through a small hallway and opened a second door.

There was a candelabrum in the hallway so that she did not even have to search for the other door.

It led directly into the Marquis's bedroom.

Instead of being asleep, as she might have expected, the Marquis was propped up against his pillows and reading a book.

As she burst into the room, he looked up in astonishment.

Gasping for breath she told him,

"Th-there is a man – climbing up outside – my bedroom window. I think it is – Monsieur Grave and he – intends to – kill me – for what I did to – them!"

The words seemed to tumble out of her mouth. For a moment the Marquis just stared at her in amazement.

Then he put down his book and got out of bed.

"I will deal with this," he said. "Stay here and don't be frightened."

He put on a dark robe that was lying on a chair and, going to a chest of drawers, took out a pistol a loaded it as Manella watched him wide-eyed and frightened.

She remembered that she had her father's duelling pistol with her, but had not thought to use it or take it with her.

The Marquis walked briskly towards the door.

"Stay here and keep Flash with you," he ordered.

"Please – be careful, my Lord – he might – hurt you," she whispered.

Even as she spoke, the Marquis had gone from the room.

She thought perhaps that he might not have heard her.

Because she felt weak and, as if her legs would no longer carry her, she sat down on the bed.

Then she put her hands over her eyes.

As if Flash sensed that something was wrong, he nuzzled against her as he did when he wanted her to pat him.

She put her arms around him.

"I am so sure he – wants to – kill me, Flash," she said. "He and the Comte will – never forgive me for – helping the – Marquis to escape from – them!"

Flash seemed to understand that she was worried and upset.

She held him closer.

At the same time she was listening carefully.

She wondered if she would be able to hear the sound of a pistol shot from so far away.

*

The Marquis walked quickly down the passage towards Manella's bedroom.

He could hardly believe that she was speaking the truth.

How could Grave be climbing up the outside of the house towards her room?

How was it possible that any man would dare to do such an appalling thing when he was resident in The Castle?

He reached the door and found that it was half-open.

His fingers tightened on the pistol.

There was no sound and he thought that she must have been mistaken for some reason.

Perhaps she had dreamt the whole thing.

It was then he heard a movement and, pushing the door open, he went in.

Manella had left the curtain drawn back.

And the moonlight revealed quite clearly the open window.

A man was climbing in through the window and already had one leg over the ledge.

He was moving so stealthily that the Marquis was aware that he was an expert burglar.

This was obviously not the first time that he had climbed up the outside of a house to get in through a window.

The Marquis stood still for a moment watching him.

Then the man slowly began to draw his other leg over the window ledge.

As he did so, the Marquis acted.

Raising up his pistol he shot the intruder not in the chest or the heart, which would have been easy, but deftly on the outside of his arm.

The explosion as he fired seemed to echo and next re-echo round the bedroom.

At the same time the man whom the Marquis had wounded gave a shrill scream and fell backwards.

Without hurrying himself, the Marquis walked across to the window and looked down at the ground.

Below him, the man, whom he had recognised as Monsieur Grave had fallen forty feet into the courtyard.

There was a flowerbed under the window and he had landed on its soft soil.

As the Marquis watched, two men then appeared from the shrubbery.

Picking up the Frenchman who was groaning in pain, they carried him to the carriage.

They were obviously afraid that they themselves might be shot at.

The two horses drawing the carriage were then driven away at full speed down the drive.

The Marquis watched them until they were completely out of sight.

Turning away from the window, he walked back the way he had come.

As he opened the door of his bedroom, Manella gave a cry and jumped up from the bed where she was still sitting with Flash ready to protect her.

"You – are – safe? You are – safe?" she stammered quickly. "They have not – hurt you?"

She flung herself against him and the Marquis put his arms around her.

Just for a moment he looked down at her.

Her eyes were dark and wide with anxiety and fear.

Her golden hair glittered in the soft candlelight as it fell over her shoulders and down her back.

Roughly he pulled her against him and his lips were on hers.

He kissed her as if he could not help himself, fiercely, demandingly and passionately.

To Manella it was as if the skies had suddenly opened to reveal an incredibly bright light.

She was instantly swept up into a Heaven that she had never known existed.

As the Marquis held her closer and closer still, his lips became even more possessive.

She felt an ecstasy sweep through her that was so wonderful that she knew it was love.

It was just as she had thought love would be, but far more marvellous.

Her whole body seemed to melt against the Marquis's so that she became a part of him and he was a part of her.

In some way that she could not understand or explain, she was his.

He kissed her until she felt as if the room whirled about them.

She was flying in the sky and was no longer on earth.

Then the Marquis raised his head.

"What have you done to me?" he asked in a hoarse voice. "I tried to prevent this from happening, but how could I know, how could I guess, that that devil would try to intrude on you?"

"D-did you – did you – kill him?" Manella asked the Marquis,

"No, but I have wounded him," the Marquis replied, "and I promise you that he will not come back."

"I-I thought he – wanted to – k-kill me." Manella murmured.

The Marquis thought, knowing Grave, he was far more likely to have wanted to kidnap her and then he would prevent her from talking of what had happened.

He would then no doubt keep her forcibly in one of the *Maisons de Plaisir* in Paris with which he was associated and keep her drugged day and night.

This, however, was not something that he could say to Manella.

It was doubtful anyway if she would understand or even want to understand the horrors that a pretty young girl could confront in Paris's lowest section of Society.

Even in the short time he had known her, the Marquis had been aware of her innocence.

Also of her ignorance of the sophisticated world that he had moved in in Paris.

A world that he knew was also waiting for him in London.

"You are quite safe, my darling," he coaxed her gently.

"I was – so frightened – for you," she murmured, "and it was – Flash who – told me that I – was in danger."

"How can this have happened to you?" the Marquis asked more of himself than her.

He kissed her again until the wonder of it was almost too marvellous to bear.

She made a little incoherent sound and hid her face against his neck.

Very gently he pulled her towards the bed.

Then he sat down and drew her to him.

"Now listen to me, my precious," he said. "I cannot let you run the risk of anything like this happening to you again. Although I think that Grave will now return to Paris and we shall not see him again, you are much too beautiful to be wandering about the world on your own."

"I don't want to – wander any further," Manella said, "I-I want to – stay here with you."

The Marquis smiled.

"That is what I want too," he said, "but it is not going to be easy for me to take care of you and therefore you have to help me."

"How – can I – help – you?" Manella asked, a puzzled expression on her face.

The Marquis drew in his breath.

"When I realised today how much I loved you," he began, "I decided that I must send you away and try my best to forget you."

Manella gave a little cry of horror.

"But *why* – why should – you want – to do that?"

The Marquis was silent for a moment before he answered her,

"Because you are so young, untouched and completely unspoilt, I thought I was doing what was best for you."

" – I don't – understand," Manella murmured.

The Marquis hesitated as if he was feeling for his words.

Then he carried on,

"I love you! I love you as I have never loved anyone before, in fact, if I was to tell the truth, I have never been in love before."

He saw the sudden radiance in Manella's eyes and continued quickly,

"But, my precious one, you must try to appreciate that I cannot ask you to marry me."

Manella was still and her eyes widened.

"I have a responsibility to my family and to my name, which has been respected all down the centuries."

He saw that Manella was listening and went on,

"I must when I marry, which will not be for many, many years, marry someone who my family will accept."

Listening, Manella felt as if a cold hand had clutched at her heart and was squeezing the lifeblood from it in a cruel manner.

"What I have decided to do," the Marquis went on, "is to protect and look after you and, of course, my beautiful one, to love you!"

Manella did not speak.

After a moment the Marquis continued,

"So I will rent a small house for you in London where we can be together whenever it is possible. And I have houses in other parts of the country where no one will ask us questions."

He paused again before he went on,

"Now I am home and the War that had seemed endless is over, I shall use my father's yacht, or else buy a new one, which will carry us to enchanted lands all over the world."

His arms drew her closer as he sighed,

"We will be very happy, my darling, and I swear to you that never again will you have to work for your living. I will provide for you so that you will have plenty of money for the rest of your life."

Manella was about to reply to him, but it was impossible as he was kissing her again.

He kissed her as if he was very excited by what he was planning and knew how happy they would be together.

He went on kissing her until it was almost impossible for her to think.

Yet she knew that she must think and think exceedingly carefully.

A thousand questions were trying to reach her lips, but the ecstasy the Marquis aroused in her was rising again.

All she could think of was him and the wonder of him.

His lips still held hers captive.

Only after what seemed a very long time did he release her and say hoarsely,

"I want to keep you with me all through night telling you how much I love you. But, my precious, I know you are tired and what has happened tonight has been a shock to you. So I am going to send you back to bed!"

He kissed her forehead before he added,

"Tomorrow. Tomorrow we will talk over our plans and make them very carefully so that no one will have the slightest idea of what is happening."

He kissed her lips.

Then resolutely, as if he ordered himself as a soldier to do his duty, he drew her across the bedroom to the little hall.

He did not open the door into the passage, but another one.

Picking up a lit candelabrum he went ahead of her into a room that Manella had not seen before.

It was very large and exquisitely furnished.

There was a huge gold carved four-poster bed that was hung with silk curtains.

"This was my mother's room," the Marquis said softly, "and you will be safe here, my darling, until the morning. Then I suggest you go back to your own room so that no one will know what has happened tonight."

He did not wait for her to agree, but set the candelabrum down beside the bed.

He took her into his arms and kissed her lips not passionately but gently, as if she was infinitely precious.

"You are mine," he asserted softly, "and I will never ever lose you."

Almost before Manella could realise what was happening, he had gone from the room.

A few seconds later she heard the door of his bedroom close.

For some minutes she could only stand rigid to the spot staring at the closed door as if she could not believe that he had left her.

Then, as she pulled back the silk cover, she found that the bed was made up.

The pillow cases were edged with Austrian lace as were the sheets and the eiderdown.

Knowing instinctively that the excitements of the evening were all over Flash grunted and settled himself down comfortably beside the bed.

Manella thought indecisively for a few moments and then climbed into it, closed her eyes and tried to think of all that had happened to her in such a short time.

The ecstasy and rapture that the Marquis had aroused in her still lingered in her breast and on her lips.

At the same time what he had just said to her was repeating itself over and over again in her mind.

It seemed to be written in the air in huge letters of fire.

What he was offering her was wrong – *wrong* and wicked.

What it meant was that, while she loved him with her heart and her soul, he did not really love her in the same way.

That was not the Heavenly love that she sought or the love that would think no sacrifice was too great.

A love that a man would die for rather than lose the perfection and glory of it.

The love that was a gift straight from God.

As she lay there still in the great bed, she knew only too well that what the Marquis was offering her was something cheap.

It was something that her mother would have thought of as a sin.

So would the Marquis's mother in whose bed she was now lying.

'I love – him! *I love – him*!' she cried out in her heart.

But her mind told her that he did not love her in the same way.

She gave a sob and then the tears began to roll down her cheeks.

*

It was not yet five o'clock when Manella, accompanied by Flash, slipped down the back stairs.

She went past the empty kitchen to the back door and let herself out.

She had lain awake for hours fighting with her conscience and her heart.

She felt it was as if her mother was guiding her and finally she knew what she must do.

'If I stay,' Manella ruminated to herself, 'because I love him, I shall either agree to what he suggests or else tell him who I am.'

She knew, if she did that, he would then feel obliged in honour to marry her.

But she also knew that he really had no wish to marry, as he had said, *'for many, many years'*.

Just as he had no wish to be drugged and then tricked into marriage by the Comtesse and her unscrupulous accomplices.

The candles were growing low when at last she made up her mind.

"We will have to go – away from – here, Flash," she told him.

Because she had spoken to him Flash pumped with his tail on the floor and she felt that he understood all that she was saying to him.

The stables were in darkness when she reached them.

She knew that, unlike at home, there would be a groom on duty.

She opened the door nearest to Heron's stall and saw by the light of the lantern hanging on the wall that most of the horses were lying down.

But Heron was standing.

She put her arms round him before she looked for his saddle.

It was with his bridle suspended on the wall opposite his stall.

Deftly, because she had done it so often, she put it on his back and fastened the girths.

She tied her small bundle of clothes to the back of the saddle as she had done when she had left home.

As if Heron was pleased at the idea of going for a ride, he tossed his head and nuzzled against her.

There was still no sign of anyone about and she guessed that the place where the groom was sleeping must be at the other end of the building.

As he was doubtless young, she expected that he would sleep, as her Nanny would have said 'like a log'.

She had remembered to bring her father's duelling pistol with her.

She tucked it with her slippers into a pocket of the saddle.

Moving as quickly and silently as she could, she took Heron out into the yard and there was a mounting-block quite near to his stall.

It took her only a second or two to settle herself onto the saddle before she picked up the reins.

With Flash running beside her, she went out of the stable and up to the front gate, which was the nearest to the main road.

The first rays of the sun were just breaking in the East and the stars were beginning to fade.

As she reached the top of the drive, she turned Heron around to look back at The Castle.

For one moment she asked herself almost savagely why she was being so foolish as to run away when she wanted so strongly to stay.

What did it matter what she did so long as she was with the Marquis?

She only wanted to be with him, to see him and to love him with all her heart and soul.

But she knew that what he wanted from her was not her soul.

If they were together under those terms, there would always be a barrier between them. It would eventually become unsurpassable and would then fall apart.

It was a barrier of his own making because he did not think that she was good enough to be his wife.

However much she might attempt to deceive herself that it did not matter, she knew that sooner or later it would poison their love for each other.

And then it would destroy it completely

She took a long last look at The Castle.

Then resolutely she rode away as quickly as she could and making for the main road.

She was running away, not only from the Marquis because of what he had suggested, but also from herself.

From a sublime love that cried out in total agony because, where he was concerned, she herself was not enough for him.

CHAPTER SEVEN

Manella rode down the narrow country lanes that twisted and turned.

She passed through several small villages without wondering if anyone was watching her progress or not.

All she could think of was the Marquis, the Marquis and the Marquis.

She felt as if every mile that separated them was like a dagger turning in her breast.

On and on she rode with determination in here eyes.

The sun rose in the sky and it became very hot.

She thought that Heron and Flash would need a rest and a drink of cool water before very long.

It was then that Manella realised that she was in a village that was much larger than those she had ridden through already.

On the far side of the village green there was a pretty black-and-white inn.

Outside it she saw that there were several men wearing top hats.

She looked at them vaguely and then was aware that they were staring at her.

She remembered and it was like a shock that she was still running away from her uncle and did not want to be seen by other people.

She next quickened Heron's pace.

As soon as they were through the village and had passed by the last thatched cottage, she turned off the road.

There was a field sloping down to some trees at the bottom of it and so she thought that there would be a small stream there.

It was just what she was looking for and she rode on.

She passed through a copse of silver birches until she found the stream, as she expected, only a short distance ahead of her.

She pulled up Heron to a standstill.

As if he understood exactly why they were there, Flash ran into the stream, standing in it, and drinking rapidly.

Manella dismounted and tied the reins onto Heron's back.

"Now go and drink," she said, "You must be thirsty and so am I for that matter."

He went ahead of her.

Because she felt hot and tired she took off her hat and put it down on the ground.

She had just done so when she heard the sound of another horse's hoofs.

Turning round she saw a man riding through the silver birches.

For a moment he was indistinct to her.

Then, as he came nearer to her, she gasped.

He was wearing a black mask and, as he then approached her, she saw to her horror that he had a pistol in his right hand.

He rode up and pulling in his horse he spoke to her in a coarse common voice,

"Just what I'm a-lookin' for! That there 'orse'll do me ever so proud it will!"

Manella gave a startled cry and, moving towards Heron, took hold of his bridle.

"You cannot take my horse," she protested loudly.

"And who's to stop me, I'd like to know?" the highwayman asked aggressively.

"I will give you money," Manella said, "everything I have, but not my horse. He is mine and I love him!"

"I'll love 'im right enough meself!" the highwayman retorted. "Now, give me the money and you can take this 'ere old crock in exchange."

He was looking Heron over as he was speaking.

Then he said,

"Come on then, you gimme 'is reins. I'll change 'orses in the wood over there and you're real damned lucky to have anyfin' to carry you!"

"I will not let you do this!" Manella stated breathlessly.

"'Ow you goin' to stop me?" the highwayman asked jeeringly.

Manella knew that even if she screamed, there would be no one to hear her.

She now wondered desperately what she could possibly do.

The highwayman was very obviously thinking over what she had told him because after a moment he demanded,

"Now then gimme the money! My needs be greater than yours be."

"Unless you promise to leave me my horse, I will not give you anything at all!" Manella replied to him defiantly.

The highwayman chuckled and it was a most unpleasant sound.

"I needs an 'orse and I needs your money too and so be quick abaht it! Give it 'ere or I'll put some lead in your dorg!"

Manella realised that she was beaten.

As she gave a murmur of horror, there was the sound of hoofs galloping towards them.

A man was coming riding through the trees.

Even before Manella could then see him clearly, he must have seen the highwayman and realised what he was doing.

He pulled a pistol from his saddle and without any warning shot at the highwayman.

It would have killed him if he had not at that very moment turned round to see who was approaching.

The bullet passed over his shoulder and the highwayman fired in return.

At the explosions of the two pistols, the horses startled,

The highwayman's horse reared, almost throwing him and so did Heron.

Manella was holding tightly onto his bridle.

But the highwayman, obviously afraid of what was happening, spurred his horse forward towards the wood.

As he rode away, Manella saw that the man who had fired at him was following him.

To her horror she then saw that it was no less than her uncle!

'He must be still searching the countryside for me and has bumped into me in this wood by sheer coincidence,' she mused to herself in terror.

He was swaying in a strange way in the saddle as he disappeared amongst the trees.

Too frightened to know what to do or even for the moment to move, she could only stare at the point in the wood where the two horses had disappeared.

Then there came another shot that seemed to reverberate through the air.

As Manella held tightly onto Heron as if for protection, yet another horse appeared, this time from the direction that she had come.

With an instant leap of her heart she saw that it was the Marquis.

He rode up to her at a gallop.

He flung himself from his horse and put his arms around her.

"Are you all right?" he asked. "You have not been hurt?"

For a moment it was impossible for Manella to speak.

She could only cling onto the Marquis knowing that, as he was there, Heron was saved.

She knew too that she wanted the Marquis more than she had ever wanted anything in the whole of her life.

"My darling, my sweet!" the Marquis was saying. "How could you leave me? How could you go away like that?"

He pulled her closer before he went on,

"Forgive me, you have to forgive me, for being such a pompous prig. I know now that I cannot possibly live without you and I want to marry you immediately."

She looked up at him in amazement, finding it hard to believe that he was actually saying the words that she so much wanted to hear.

She was not quite certain if she was imagining it.

Her eyes were now filling with tears and her lips were trembling.

The Marquis looked down at her, thinking that no woman could ever look lovelier.

Then he said softly,

"I will ask you properly, hoping that you will forgive me. Will you, my lovely, precious, perfect little angel from Heaven, do me the great honour of becoming my wife?"

He spoke solemnly, but he did not wait for an answer.

His lips were on hers and he kissed her wildly, passionately and demandingly.

Manella felt that this must be a dream and could not really be happening to her.

How was it true?

After her running away and being very frightened by the highwayman, was the Marquis really there and asking her to be his wife?

It was so wonderful and at the same time so extraordinary!

She felt herself trembling against him and had the strange feeling that he was trembling too.

He raised his head and said in a hoarse voice,

"I thought I had lost you! I saw you going down the drive as dawn broke and could not believe that you were really leaving me. I had thought conceitedly that you loved me."

"I-I *do* – love you," Manella replied in a whisper, "but I – knew that it was wrong to do – what you wanted of me."

"Completely and absolutely wrong!" the Marquis agreed positively. "And I realised as I watched you go that I had destroyed my only real hope of happiness in my life."

He kissed her again as if it was easier to tell her what she meant to him without words.

They clung together as if they could never be parted.

Then Manella looked up and saw a horse coming out of the wood.

As it drew nearer, she gave an exclamation.

"It is Magpie!"

The Marquis, who had his back to the approaching horse, turned his head.

"How do you know?" he asked. "Surely this is not the horse that the highwayman was riding?"

Even as he spoke, Magpie reached them and Heron whinnied as if greeting him.

It was then that the Marquis realised that the two horses looked very much alike.

The new horse was as well-bred and good-looking as Heron.

Manella went over to Magpie and patted him on the neck.

She saw that the reins hung loose and so she knotted them at his neck.

The Marquis watched her for a moment.

And then he asked her,

"As you seem to know this horse, perhaps you would tell me who it belongs to?"

Manella drew in a deep breath.

"I-It belongs to my uncle," she responded. "It is he I am – running – away from and if – Magpie has unseated him – I must get away – at once."

As she spoke, her voice was trembling and she then looked in the direction that Magpie had come from.

There was no sign of her uncle.

Then, as if she suddenly realised that she need no longer be afraid, she moved closer to the Marquis.

"Will you – tell him that I am – staying with you and that – we are going to – be m-married?"

She spoke the words slowly and tentatively as if she was half-afraid that they might not be true.

"I will tell him you belong to me," the Marquis answered, "and I cannot imagine that he will object to our marriage,"

It flashed through Manella's mind that, if she married the Marquis, her uncle would not find it at all easy to blackmail him into paying his debts.

There was, however, no point in her saying so.

She could only pray that somehow the Marquis would prevent her uncle from bullying her.

And most of all from having to marry the old Duke of Dunster.

It all seemed confused and unreal in her mind after the shock of what had just occurred.

But there was also the wonder and ecstasy of knowing that the Marquis really loved her after all and wants to marry her.

He had actually asked her to marry him without knowing who she was!

As if he understood what she was thinking, the Marquis suggested gently,

"Leave everything to me. I will go and see what has happened to your uncle while you stay here and take charge of the horses."

He kissed her first as if he could not help himself.

Mounting his horse, he rode off deeper into the wood.

Manella watched him go.

And then she was saying a deep prayer of gratitude to God because he loved her.

At the same time it was a cry for help in case her uncle should be unpleasant and hostile.

Worst of all his behaviour might be so repulsive that the Marquis would regret having asked her to be his wife.

'Help me – God, help me – Mama.' she begged. 'The Marquis has – found me and he really – loves me! Please, oh – *please* – don't let anything – spoil it now!'

The two horses were now cropping the grass quietly and Flash was again standing in the stream as if he still wanted to cool himself down.

Manella moved instinctively a little way towards the part of the wood that the Marquis had just vanished into.

She was still praying.

She was so afraid that at any moment he might appear with her uncle and that he was determined to make trouble.

After what seemed to her a very long time, she saw the Marquis returning.

He was alone!

As he came through the trees, she could not look at his face, afraid of what she would see there.

She just stood waiting.

He reached her, dismounted at once and put his arms around her.

He held her close, but he did not kiss her.

After a moment Manella asked in a voice that he could hardly hear,

"W-what – has h-happened?"

"I am afraid, my darling," the Marquis replied, "that your uncle is dead!"

"Dead?"

Manella could hardly repeat the word.

"The highwayman had shot him right through the heart," the Marquis explained, "and there was another wound on his left shoulder where he must have hit him the first time that he fired his pistol."

Manella closed her eyes tightly and hid her face against his shoulder.

"There is nothing we can do for him now," the Marquis said quietly, "and because I do not want you to be upset, I think it would be best if we went straight to the Chief Constable, who was a friend of my father's, and tell him exactly what has occurred her in this wood."

"Y-you don't – want to move – Uncle Herbert's body?" Manella asked.

"No," the Marquis said firmly. "I don't want you to be upset by seeing him and, as I have already told you, there is nothing we can do. The bullet passed through his heart. He would have died instantly."

He did not wait for Manella to reply, but lifted her onto Heron's back.

Then he untied the reins that she had knotted on Magpie's neck.

Leading him, he mounted Tempest and started to ride back through the trees towards the village.

Flash followed behind them dutifully.

Manella thought that it was significant that for the first time since she had run away there was no need for her to hurry.

She looked at the Marquis and he smiled at her.

"I love and adore you!" he said softly, "and when we get back to The Castle, I will be able to tell you just how much."

She smiled back at him.

As they rode on together, she thought that the sun had never been more golden and the air so fresh and invigorating.

With the Marquis beside her, it was as if they were riding a golden road to Paradise.

As they next approached the village, there seemed to be no one about except for some children who were playing happily on the green.

To her surprise the Marquis stopped.

"I want to thank you," he said to them, "for being so clever as to tell me where this lady had gone and that there was a wicked highwayman hiding among the trees. Go now and buy yourselves all the sweets you want and here is the money to pay for them."

He took a purse from his pocket and gave each of the smaller children a half-sovereign piece and to the older ones he gave a guinea.

They stared down at the money in their hands as if completely mesmerised and far too excited to thank him.

They rode on and then after a long silence Manella wavered in a small voice,

"If they – had not told you – where I was – the highwayman – would have – taken Heron from me."

"Your uncle might have prevented it," the Marquis said, "but I cannot understand why, when he had his pistol in his hand, he did not at least disable the highwayman."

"Papa always said that Uncle Herbert was not a good shot!" Manella replied. "It annoyed him that his brother preferred London to the country."

"I don't think I have ever seen your uncle before," the Marquis remarked.

He was thinking as he spoke that he looked an unpleasant individual and he could well understand why Manella had been so frightened of him.

They rode on for a little while until the Marquis said,

"The Chief Constable lives only about a mile away from here, so we will call on him on our way to The Castle. You must tell me, my precious one, what is your uncle's name and if, as I suspect, you are not 'Miss Chinon', what is yours?"

Manella gave a little impromptu laugh.

"It seems – so strange – but very very – wonderful – that you really want to – marry me – not knowing who I am."

"I knew as I saw you going down the drive at dawn this morning that, if you were the Devil's daughter, I would still want to make you my wife!" the Marquis explained.

Manella drew in her breath.

"If you only – knew how – much I have – longed to hear you say – that."

"Now tell me who you are," the Marquis ordered, "and what is the name of your uncle."

"He was the seventh – Earl of Avondale," Manella whispered. "He was – Papa's brother and inherited the title because – I was the only child."

Manella hesitated before continuing,

"I was running away from him because, being in debt, he was trying to force me to marry a rich old man, the Duke of Dunster."

The Marquis stared at her in sheer astonishment.

"But I knew your father when I was a boy!" he exclaimed. "My father was very fond of him. Why did you not tell me?"

Manella turned away from him and did not reply.

"I know the answer," the Marquis said. "Because you were hiding you called yourself by a French name."

"I-It was my – grandmother's name," Manella sighed.

"And when I offered you my protection," the Marquis said slowly, as if he was working it out, "you thought that I did not really love you."

Again there was nothing that Manella could say.

The Marquis drew his horse a little nearer to hers.

"It was incredibly stupid of me," he said, "not to know that any woman as perfect and as sublime asyou must have come from a family the equal of my own."

He paused before he added,

"I can only admit that I am utterly ashamed of myself for my lack of perception in not realising how unique and wonderful you are and for thinking even for a moment that I could be happy without you as my wife."

The way he spoke was very moving and Manella said,

"Please – do not let us talk about it any – more. I love you – and now that you – love me I am so happy that I – feel I want to – fly into the sky like a bird."

There was a note of sheer rapture in her voice and she added,

"I want – to forget – everything that has – frightened me."

"I will make sure of that'" the Marquis promised her.

Because of the way he was looking at her, Manella felt her heart turn over in her breast.

*

Later on that night, Manella lay once again in the big gold-canopied bed that had always been occupied by the Marchionesses of Buckingdon.

She was waiting for her husband to come through the communicating door.

It was proving difficult for her to believe that she really was married.

The Marquis had arranged everything.

He had seen the Chief Constable as soon as he could and had related the whole story to him and he had then told him not to worry.

He would send his men to find the Earl's body and then have it taken to the Church at Avondale to await burial.

It was as they were riding back that the Marquis said,

"You know, my precious darling, that the only sensible thing for us to do is be married immediately, in fact this very evening."

Manella looked at him in astonishment and he explained,

"Your uncle, appalling though I realise he was, had become on your father's death the Head of the Family. So all your relations must be notified at once in case they wish to attend the funeral."

He paused for a moment, as if he was thinking it out, before he went on,

"It means that we cannot be together in the same house without a chaperone. It will be expected by your family that many months of mourning must pass before I can make you my bride."

"I-I don't – want to – leave you," Manella murmured softly.

"It is something I will never allow you to do," he answered her, "and, as my Chapel is Private and the Vicar of the Parish is my Chaplain too, I can marry without the necessity of a Special Licence."

Manella was aware that this applied to a number of Chapels and the one in Mayfair was notorious for the number of marriages that took place there.

As they rode side by side, the Marquis put out his hand.

"Will you marry me at once, my darling?" he asked. "Otherwise we may have to wait a long time before we can go on our honeymoon. Not that it would matter where we were so long as we could be together and in each other's arms."

Manella felt his fingers press hers and she said,

"I would be happy with you on – top of the – Himalayas or at the bottom of the – sea!"

The Marquis laughed.

"I cannot promise you a journey to the bottom of the sea, but I will most certainly take you to India as well as to a great number of other places where I will tell you over and over again of my endless and strong love for you."

He paused and then added softly,

"We will be certain that we have been there before and have loved each other in other lives."

"That – is what – I believe too," Manella exclaimed, "but I never – imagined I would – find someone – who thought the way – I do."

"We think the same, our love is the same, and we are one and the same!" the Marquis declared.

As The Castle came into sight Manella said,

"I suppose you realise that I have very few clothes with me and I am afraid you will find me not at all smart. I – shall compare very unfavourably with the – elegant ladies – who have amused you in – Paris and London."

"Whatever you wear you look beautiful and I will see nothing but your eyes and your lips," the

Marquis replied. "However I am planning to send Wilson to London tomorrow to tell all the top dressmakers to bring us their prettiest gowns for you to choose from."

"Will – they really – agree to come?" Manella asked.

"I will be very surprised if they do not jump at the chance," the Marquis said, his eyes twinkling.

"Of course. I had forgotten how – important you are!" Manella replied.

The Marquis thought that it was something that no other woman would have forgotten and he understood what Manella meant.

She loved him simply as a man and that was how he had always wanted to be loved.

And he loved her because he had never met anyone like her and never would.

She was pure, unspoilt and, in every way he could think of, completely perfect.

When they arrived back at The Castle, he took her up to his mother's bedroom.

"This is yours," he said, "and, my precious, no Countess has ever been as beautiful as the first Marchioness will be."

"As long as – you think I am – beautiful," Manella said, "nothing – else matters."

He kissed her tenderly and then left her.

The housekeeper was wildly excited by the information that they were to be married and produced all sorts of things to make Manella feel like a bride.

The Marquis's Chaplain arrived at half-past-six. By that time Manella was dressed in her own white muslin gown.

But she wore a magnificent Brussels lace veil and a large tiara of diamonds.

She was told that it had been worn by the last six Countesses on their Wedding Day.

Her bouquet was of orchids and lilies, which came from the greenhouse.

When the Marquis brought her to the Chapel, she saw at once that it was decorated with the same flowers.

The only witnesses were Mrs. Franklin and Dobbins and, of course, Flash.

It was obvious that the two servants both felt very honoured to be allowed to take part in the proceedings.

After the Marriage Service had taken place, during which Manella felt that the angels of Heaven were singing a celestial anthem, they went up to her boudoir.

It was a lovely room that she had not seen before.

There were three windows to illuminate the many treasures that successive Chatelaines of The Castle had accumulated over many centuries.

It was decorated with the same flowers that were in her bouquet and her bedroom.

She thought that the gardeners must have emptied the conservatory and the greenhouses.

They toasted themselves in champagne during a light dinner.

Manella guessed that it had been put together with the greatest difficulty, but with a loving endeavour, by Bessie and Jane and doubtless all the rest of the household all helped.

It was not a French meal, but it was very palatable.

She knew, however, that she and the Marquis would feel that anything at this moment would taste like the Ambrosia of the Gods.

When the meal was over, the Marquis drew her into the bedroom.

Manella had removed her veil and tiara before sitting down to dinner.

Now the Marquis removed the pins from her hair so that it cascaded over her shoulders.

He pulled her into his arms and kissed her gently.

She felt a wild exhilarating excitement sweep through her body.

He undid the buttons of her gown without releasing her lips.

Then he raised his head and said with a voice that was very deep,

"Get into bed, my wonderful wife."

A little later he came into the room and, sitting down on the side of the bed, he looked down at her.

"Are you really real?" he asked.

"That is – what I was – about to ask you," Manella answered. "I am – so afraid that this is a – dream and I will – wake up to find I am still – running away from – Uncle Herbert – because of his determination to make me – marry the Duke!"

"Instead you are married to me!" the Marquis asserted. "And just as I know I am the first man ever to have kissed you, my darling, I know that there will never be any other man in your life."

He climbed into the bed beside her as he spoke and took her into his arms.

"I love you so desperately," he now said, "and so overwhelmingly that I am afraid of frightening you or hurting you."

Manella was quivering because his hands were touching her.

Then, as he kissed her eyes, both her cheeks, her mouth, her neck and the softness of her breasts, she knew that she was in Heaven.

She felt the warmth of the sun and the shining of the stars in her body.

The moonlight too was moving through her and she was no longer human but Divine.

Then, as the Marquis made her his very gently and lovingly, together they touched the peaks of ecstasy.

Made in United States
North Haven, CT
21 March 2023

34386693R00104